THE WRATH OF THE LIZARD LORD

JON MAYHEW

BLOOMSBURY

LONDON   NEW DELHI   NEW YORK   SYDNEY

For Sarah Davies

Bloomsbury Publishing, London, New Delhi, New York and Sydney

First published in Great Britain in June 2014 by Bloomsbury Publishing Plc
50 Bedford Square, London WC1B 3DP

www.bloomsbury.com
www.JonMayhewBooks.com

Bloomsbury is a registered trademark of Bloomsbury Publishing Plc

A CIP catalogue record for this book is available from the British Library

ISBN 978 1 4088 2632 4

1 3 5 7 9 10 8 6 4 2

Typeset by Hewer Text UK Ltd, Edinburgh
Printed and bound in Great Britain by CPI Group (UK) Ltd, Croydon CR0 4YY

'But a man, a living man, and with him a whole generation of gigantic animals. Buried in the entrails of the earth – it was too monstrous to be believed!'

Jules Verne, *A Journey to the Centre of the Earth*

ELBA,
1815

CHAPTER ONE
A DEMON FROM HELL

Dakkar bit his lip, hardly daring to breathe as he approached the guard who was slumped against the tunnel wall. Crimson blood stained the white of the man's shredded uniform and a pistol shook in his hand. He lay beside a solid oak door that led deeper into the building's cellars or perhaps up to the ground floor. The remains of another door littered the other end of the passage. It had been smashed open with some force.

'Oginski, quickly!' Dakkar hissed to his mentor, who followed behind him in the tunnel. 'Someone got here before us!'

Oginski barged past, his big frame almost crushing Dakkar against the rough side of the passageway. He snatched a flaming torch from a bracket in the wall and squatted down beside the guard. Dakkar joined him.

'Who did this, mon ami?' Oginski said to the guard as he gingerly examined the man's wounds.

'A demon!' the guard gasped, his eyes widening. He lifted his pistol and waved it towards the shattered door that had once barred the tunnel that stretched before them. 'I shot it and it fled back from whence it came. Down there.'

The whole tunnel shook as a roar echoed around them.

'It hasn't gone!' Dakkar yelled. 'Is this loaded?' he demanded, grabbing the guard's rifle. The man gave a weary nod and slumped back as if passing all responsibility to the new stranger.

'Dakkar, wait!' Oginski called after him, but Dakkar had already dashed through the splintered door. With an oath, he charged after him.

Oginski's torch cast wild, dancing shadows, the light reflecting off a trail of black blood spots that led down the tunnel.

'Whatever it is, it's bleeding,' he called to Oginski. 'Do demons bleed?'

'Demons!' Oginski spat. 'Whatever came down here is as mortal as you. Which is why you should *slow down!*'

'Look!' Dakkar cried, hurrying ahead.

In the flickering light, Dakkar glimpsed the glowing orb of an eye and a flickering tip of a tail. Torchlight shimmered on the creature's scaly skin and flashed on rows of pointed yellow teeth. Then it vanished round the corner.

Dakkar stopped so abruptly that Oginski ran into his back, sending them both sprawling to the ground.

'Impetuous boy!' Oginski groaned, rolling on to all fours. 'What do you think you're doing?'

Dakkar staggered to his feet, rubbing his bruised back-side. He stared up at the bend in the tunnel.

'Didn't you see it?' he asked, his voice low.

'See what?' Oginski snapped, dusting himself down.

'The demon?' Dakkar whispered.

Oginski stepped in front of Dakkar and grabbed him by the shoulders. 'Dakkar,' he said, staring deep into the boy's eyes. 'There is no demon.'

'But I saw it,' Dakkar began. 'It was a monster . . . with teeth and tail, scales and claws.'

'Follow me,' Oginski said, blowing his breath through his teeth and shaking his head. 'And keep that rifle ready.'

The silence was unbearable as they inched towards the blind turn in the tunnel. *What is that thing?* thought Dakkar. *It might be waiting to pounce even now.*

Rock dust began to trickle from the ceiling, making Dakkar freeze.

'Oginski,' he hissed. 'The tunnel, it's –'

But Dakkar's voice was drowned out by the deafening roar of tumbling rock. He stumbled to the side as chunks of stone rained down. One rock struck him, numbing his shoulder. He could see Oginski falling backward through a fog of dust as the entire passageway shook. Bigger slabs crashed around him, and Dakkar crouched, covering his head with his hands as if that would save him somehow.

Then all fell still.

Oginski coughed and spluttered as the air cleared. 'Are you all right, Dakkar?'

'Yes,' Dakkar said, his voice parched by the experience. 'Just a bit bruised.'

'We can't follow it now,' Oginski said. 'Whatever it was.'

Rubble covered the ground and a wall of fallen stone sealed the tunnel ahead of them. Nothing was coming out of there.

Dakkar peered over Oginski's shoulder.

'Listen!' Oginski said, holding up a hand. A faint, metallic whine, followed by a grating, scraping sound from behind the rock, gradually died away.

'I've heard that sound before,' Dakkar said, shivering suddenly and hugging the rifle against his chest. 'It was a Mole Machine. Do you think another of your brothers has perfected such a device?'

He thought back to their last encounter with Count Cryptos. He had been building a giant machine that dug tunnels, intending to cause a massive volcanic explosion. Thankfully, Oginski and Dakkar had foiled the plot but Count Cryptos had died in the ensuing chaos. There would be another Count Cryptos to take his place, though – that was certain. The count who had died was one of Oginski's six brothers, all of whom were determined to change the world order and rule themselves.

'I fear it's more than possible,' Oginski said, snapping Dakkar out of his thoughts. 'One of my wonderful brothers must be behind this. We were right to come and investigate.'

'Do you think Count Cryptos brought the . . . thing here?' Dakkar asked, edging towards the pile of stones and straining to hear.

'Whatever-it-was came up into this cellar through a tunnel made by the Mole Machine,' Oginski muttered, dabbing a finger in the congealing blood on the floor. 'When it went back, the tunnel collapsed behind it. We can't linger – the alarm will have been raised by now.'

'You think the one we came for has already escaped?' Dakkar said.

'I don't know but that tremor and the wounded man are enough to bring him *and* his entire personal guard down here if he hasn't left already.'

As if in reply to Oginski's comment, muffled shouts echoed down the tunnel towards them, followed by the sound of urgent footsteps.

'We'd better go!' Dakkar said, turning to hurry back up the passage.

Something gleamed in the frame of the shattered door as Dakkar passed it, making him stop and squint in the dim light.

'Dakkar, there is no time,' Oginski snapped.

'It's a claw,' Dakkar exclaimed, plucking it from the wood of the door. 'It must be two inches long!'

'Very good,' Oginski said, grabbing Dakkar's arm. 'We can look at it later. Now, come!'

Dakkar slipped the claw into his pocket and scurried after him.

The wounded guard still lay propped against the wall. His breathing was shallow and blood pooled around him. Dakkar felt a lump in his throat.

'You never get used to it,' Oginski said, his voice heavy. 'If you do then you've become a monster.'

'Halt!'

Dakkar spun round and found himself staring down the barrel of a rifle. Three guards, in similar blue and white uniform to the dying man, spilled through the remaining doorway, glaring at them with bayonets fixed.

'Gentlemen, it is not what you think,' Oginski said in fluent French.

'This man will vouch for us,' Dakkar said, glancing down at the injured guard.

But the guard gave a last, strangled gasp and sagged lifeless against the wall.

'My comrade seems indisposed to answer any questions,' the head guard hissed, clicking back the flintlock on his rifle. 'And I see no other possible culprits. Prepare to die.'

CHAPTER TWO
THE LITTLE CORPORAL

The other two guards cocked their rifles and levelled them at Dakkar and Oginski.

'You must listen to us,' Dakkar said, shaking his fists in desperation. 'We didn't kill this man.'

'Even if that were so,' the guard said, squinting down the rifle at Dakkar, 'you are trespassing beneath the palace of the emperor himself!'

More footsteps echoed through the tunnel. Dakkar squeezed his eyes tight shut, waiting for the roar of the rifles.

An imperious voice cut through the tramp of feet. 'Wait!'

Dakkar opened one eye to see the tunnel filled with men in blue and white uniforms. The soldiers who had first apprehended them lowered their weapons and stood to attention.

A stocky man worked his way through the scrum, soldiers standing bolt upright as he did so. His clothes – a brown woollen jacket, green waistcoat and cream knee breeches – suggested to Dakkar that he was a gentleman of some kind, while his steely blue eyes suggested a higher authority. He reminded Dakkar of his own father, the Rajah of Bundelkhand, and hoped he wasn't such a ruthless and pitiless ruler.

'Count Oginski,' the man said, a smile lengthening his round face. 'Is this a social call or have you come to join me?'

'Your excellency,' Oginski said, giving a shallow bow. 'I've come to save your life.'

'Really?' The man seemed amused by this. His eyes wandered to Dakkar. 'You bring a child on your rescue mission?'

'Forgive me, your excellency,' Oginski said, gesturing to Dakkar. 'This is Prince Dakkar of Bundelkhand.'

'And I'm not a child,' Dakkar said, glaring back at the man.

Dakkar felt Oginski's elbow in his ribs and suppressed a gasp.

'This,' Oginski said through gritted teeth, 'is the Emperor Napoleon.'

Dakkar felt the blood drain from his face. He'd seen pictures of Napoleon Bonaparte in British newspapers – caricatures, he realised now – looking short, in ridiculously oversized uniforms. Dakkar had heard people call him 'the Little Corporal' but this man was no shorter than most of the soldiers that surrounded him.

He knows Oginski, Dakkar thought. *How?*

Napoleon stared deep into Dakkar's eyes. Dakkar felt his cheeks redden again.

'A boy,' Napoleon murmured, 'from a minor principality in a huge country. Did they mock you at school, boy? Did they laugh at your accent?'

Dakkar nodded dumbly. He felt as if Napoleon could see into his soul.

'My own family were Corsican nobles,' he said, his voice quiet. 'They mocked me at school too. It drove me to greater things.'

'I ran away,' Dakkar murmured, avoiding Napoleon's searching gaze.

'Sometimes, that is wise,' Napoleon said, with a smirk. Then his smile faded as he looked down on the fallen guard. 'Who did this, Oginski?'

'I'm not certain,' Oginski said, his voice hoarse.

'He told us he saw a demon,' Dakkar said, without thinking. 'We saw something too, through there, but the tunnel collapsed.'

'A demon?' Napoleon raised an eyebrow.

'It was a beast of some kind. We think Count Cryptos might have been behind this,' Oginski said, his voice heavy with resignation. Clearly, he had wanted to avoid giving too much detail away.

'I would concur with you,' Napoleon replied, clicking his fingers.

An old man in uniform hurried forward. Despite his limp and his grey hair, Dakkar could tell he was still a strong man – and probably a deadly fighter. The old man pulled a scrap of black cloth from his pocket and handed it to Napoleon with a curt bow.

Napoleon held the cloth up to examine it. It was a badge with a snake curled round the letter C and a trident poking up behind it.

Dakkar recognised the emblem. It was the insignia of Oginski's brother Count Cryptos, who had tried to kidnap and finally kill them. But Count Cryptos was more than just one person – Oginski had five other brothers, each dedicated to the cause of world domination, all of them working together secretly to bring down the great nations of man.

'Alfonse here encountered three of Cryptos's men in the tunnels this morning,' Napoleon said, giving a grim smile. 'Or rather they encountered Alfonse.'

The old man's weather-beaten face cracked into a broad grin and the soldiers around them chuckled.

Dakkar shivered.

'It is the Cryptos insignia,' Oginski murmured. 'My sources told me that my brothers were trying to get to you.'

'Your sources are reliable,' Napoleon said, nodding. 'They have been probing our defences for some time now but you need not fear for me. I am well protected by my Imperial Guard.' He gestured to the soldiers who flanked him.

'Cryptos has ways of getting around that protection, your excellency,' Oginski said, giving a tight smile. 'They are not to be underestimated.'

Dakkar looked from Oginski to Napoleon and back again, marvelling at how, a moment ago, they were about to be shot and now they were talking with Napoleon as if he were an old friend.

'Oginski and I go back a long way,' Napoleon said, addressing Dakkar directly. 'We have fought with and against each other in the past.'

'In my wilder days,' Oginski muttered, lowering his gaze to the ground. He looked up at Napoleon. 'We have both changed since then!'

For a moment Napoleon and Oginski stared at each other. Dakkar glanced from one to the other, trying to read their faces. Finally, Napoleon shook himself and clapped his hands.

'I know the dangers of Cryptos, Oginski, which is why I am leaving,' he said, still clasping his hands together. 'I am returning to Paris. My people need me. Join us!'

'That would be an honour, your excellency,' Oginski said, then nodded at Dakkar, 'but I have responsibilities now. I'm not the firebrand you once knew and you yourself seem somehow . . . changed.'

'I'm not sure what you mean,' Napoleon said. He patted his round stomach and gave a laugh. 'I suppose none of us is getting any younger, that is true.'

'But if you leave this island,' Dakkar blurted out before he could stop himself, 'won't people try to catch you?'

Napoleon shrugged. 'They may,' he said, 'but I'd rather die than watch my once great nation be torn apart and its citizens treated like dogs.'

'I think we have wasted enough of your excellency's time,' Oginski said suddenly, giving a shuffling bow as he backed away. 'With your permission, we will depart.'

'No,' Napoleon said, narrowing his eyes. 'You shall stay a little longer. I have many questions to ask and I suspect you may be of some assistance. You always had an inventive mind. You were also very friendly with one Robert Fulton, the man who tried to impress us with his submersible craft, were you not?'

Dakkar shifted uncomfortably and looked up at Oginski, whose face had paled.

'I n-no longer dabble in engineering and natural philosophy,' he stammered. 'I am more of a poet these days.'

'Then we shall discuss poetry and great literature,' Napoleon said, clapping his hands. 'And maybe your young companion can shed some light on how you managed to get into the cellars beneath my home without having to overpower even one of my men.'

'Please, your excellency –' Oginski began.

'Enough of this charade,' Napoleon snapped. 'I suspect there is more to you and your young friend than meets the eye, Oginski. Guards, take them to the cells!'

The soldiers sprang into action and before Dakkar could act, firm hands clasped his arms and a gun barrel jabbed painfully in his ribs. Oginski's protests were useless as they were marched away from Napoleon and down the tunnel towards imprisonment.

CHAPTER THREE
TOYS

Dakkar's rasping breath was all but drowned out by the clatter of the soldiers' hobnail boots on the rough tunnel floor. Every now and then, Oginski would utter an oath and Dakkar heard him groan as a guard jabbed him with a rifle butt.

'And things were going so well,' Dakkar hissed. 'I thought you and Bonaparte were friends.'

'We were,' Oginski said, his voice breathless.

'How long will he keep us?' Dakkar asked.

'You won't be here long, mes amis,' said Alfonse, the old guard. 'We leave for France in the evening. Napoleon will have decided what to do with you by then. Either you'll be free or your worries will be over.' The wrinkles on his tanned face deepened with his grin. Dakkar's scalp prickled.

Five guards had jostled them away to the cells, led by Alfonse, who now stopped outside a heavily studded iron door.

Dakkar took in its dimensions at a glance. Two inches thick. Blast proof. A small grille at the top for observation and a food hatch at the bottom. Bolted from the outside: no chance to pick a lock. *Once we're inside that cell, we're trapped*, he thought.

The tunnel had widened at this point and there was a small table and a seat for whoever guarded the cells. Another studded door faced the one that awaited Dakkar and Oginski.

'If you could empty your pockets, gentlemen,' Alfonse said, and gestured to the table.

Dakkar glanced over at Oginski, who, after a jab with a rifle, disgorged a small pistol, some gold coin and a snuffbox from his coat and slammed them on the table.

'And you, young man,' Alfonse said with a nod at Dakkar.

Dakkar pulled out string, old cogs from a broken clock, some nails and a metal object shaped rather like a toy dog. A key poked from its side.

'What is this?' Alfonse sneered, picking up the toy dog. 'You are a little old for wind-up toys, are you not?'

'Please, monsieur, be careful with that,' Dakkar said, reaching out. 'It is . . . fragile. If you overwind it, the spring might break.'

'Pah!' Alfonse said, giving the toy's key a few savage twists. 'A grown boy playing with mechanical animals!'

He turned to his comrades and placed the toy dog on the table. They gathered round as the dog began to totter towards the edge of the table top, the sound of the spring whirring. One of the men poked it just as it teetered on the brink of the table, sending it marching back towards Alfonse.

'Six, five, four . . .' Dakkar muttered under his breath.

'Why are you count–' Alfonse started.

Before he could finish his question, Dakkar shoulder-charged Oginski, sending him tumbling into the cell. The tunnel erupted in a storm of fire and smoke and Dakkar barely had time to dive inside. Oginski threw himself against the iron door and heaved his back against the blast that tried to ram it open again.

Dakkar's ears rang and his head thumped. The echo of the blast rumbled through the tunnel, fading into silence. Oginski swayed in front of Dakkar for a moment and then staggered. Dakkar leapt up to grab him.

'Clockwork explosives?' Oginski croaked, peering at Dakkar as if he were far off. 'When did you think that one up?'

'Just something I've been playing about with.' Dakkar gave a grin and held Oginski upright as the man slumped against him. 'Oginski, we must hurry,' he said, shaking the heavy man's shoulders.

Outside, Alfonse and the men groaned, their faces blackened with gunpowder. Dakkar could see their belongings scattered across the tunnel.

'Thank goodness,' Dakkar said, his voice barely a whisper. 'The blast wasn't enough to kill – it just stunned them.'

'Good lad,' Oginski said, leaning awkwardly against the tunnel wall.

Dakkar stooped down to rescue Oginski's pistol and snuffbox, which lay among the debris. They hurried down the tunnel, clutching a guttering torch that had stayed alight somehow. Dakkar glanced over his shoulder at Oginski's pale face.

'Are you all right?' Dakkar called back.

'Yes,' Oginski said, stumbling against the passage walls. 'Keep going!'

Behind them distant voices barked commands and shouts of alarm grew louder. Dakkar scurried back to Oginski as the big man tripped and fell heavily.

'Not far now,' Dakkar panted, heaving him to his feet.

'I can't,' Oginski panted. 'Leave me. Get the *Nautilus* away from here . . . You need to warn the world about Bonaparte . . .'

'You can do that yourself.' Dakkar grunted and slung Oginski's arm over his shoulder, half dragging him along the passage. 'I'm not leaving you.'

The voices were close now. Oginski stopped again and leaned against the wall of the tunnel.

'Snuffbox,' he said in a hoarse whisper.

'What?' Dakkar snapped. 'Oginski, this is no time –'

'Snuffbox,' Oginski repeated, extending a shaking hand. 'You're not the only one with a trick up his sleeve.'

Dakkar pulled the snuffbox from his pocket and handed it over. Shadows wobbled in the torchlight as the pursuers grew nearer.

'Just something . . . *I've* been playing . . . about with,' Oginski said, giving Dakkar a feeble grin. He flicked a lever from the side of the box and hurled it down the tunnel, stumbling back as he did.

The box hit the ground with a metallic clank and the tunnel behind them began to fill with a thick brown smoke. Dakkar grinned at the shouts of consternation, and even a gunshot that split the air, as the guards stumbled to a halt.

He turned to see Oginski almost falling forward down the passage. Hurrying after, Dakkar grabbed his arm once more and began scanning the sides of the tunnel, which were becoming rougher and rockier as they descended into the labyrinth that lay beneath the cellars and passageways. But the cries of the guards grew louder once more. In a few minutes, they would be upon Dakkar.

A musket ball buzzed past Dakkar's ear and ricocheted off the tunnel wall. Dakkar groped along the wall, his heart hammering. *It has to be here. Surely this is where we broke into the tunnel.*

Finally, he found a narrow crevice. Grabbing Oginski, Dakkar pushed him into the gap, gripping his upper arm tightly. Another shot rang against the wall close by, sending splinters of stone showering on to them. For a moment, rock scraped Oginski's shoulders and Dakkar feared he would be stuck. Then the big man slipped through and vanished. Dakkar winced at the heavy thud that followed and even managed a grin at Oginski's muffled oath.

Footsteps clattered down the passage and Dakkar pushed himself through the gap, briefly relishing the cool rock against his skin.

The slap and gurgle of waves against rock echoed around Dakkar's aching ears. Nearby, the *Nautilus* bobbed in the water. Grey light filtering in from the mouth of the cave glimmered on her polished planks and the bands of brass that held them tight. A long tube of burnished wood with a short stubby tower halfway along, she made Dakkar think of a wooden whale waiting impatiently for their return. She looked like no other boat on earth. This was Oginski's submarine, an incredible craft that could submerge underwater and take them to places mankind had never seen before.

Revived by the cool air, Oginski crawled on all fours across the rough rock towards the moored submarine. A rattle of metal warned Dakkar that the guards were uncomfortably close. He glanced back to see a gun barrel poking through the crevice, then another and another.

As he sprinted to the submarine, Dakkar bent down and dragged Oginski to his feet. Together they slipped and slithered up the ladder to the top of the tower.

The sea cavern exploded in a blaze of gunfire and musket balls buzzed around his ears. A bullet nicked the rim of Dakkar's ear and smacked into Oginski's shoulder. Blood speckled Dakkar's face and stung his eyes.

'Oginski!' Dakkar yelled, and pushed his mentor into the hatch at the top, rolling in after him.

With a cry, Dakkar tumbled headlong into the stuffy closeness of the *Nautilus*'s tower and landed with a thump on top of Oginski. Peering through the porthole in the tower, Dakkar could see the guards squirming to get through the crevice. Fortunately, in their eagerness to capture Dakkar and Oginski, three of them had tried to get through at once, becoming wedged.

Clambering up the interior ladder, Dakkar slammed the hatch shut and then hurried back down to Oginski. He lay groaning, blood staining his shoulder.

'Are you badly hurt?' Dakkar asked, kneeling beside Oginski.

'No time,' Oginski groaned. 'Get the *Nautilus* . . . away.'

Oginski was right. The men would disentangle themselves and clamber on to the sub at any moment.

Dakkar rushed over to the controls and the captain's seat that sat at the base of the tower. He grabbed the craft's wheel and turned the disc in the centre. Behind him the engine began to hum. This was the Voltalith coming to life, a fragment of the Eye of Neptune, a supercharged electric rock that powered the craft. Dakkar had been forced to retrieve it from the ocean bed by the last Count Cryptos.

Something cracked above Dakkar's head. A musket ball lodged itself in the planks of the tower. Dakkar prayed that it hadn't broken the watertight seal. He slammed the craft's drive lever into *Backwater* and slowly the *Nautilus* began to reverse away from the rocky shore of the cave and into the sea pool. Dakkar knew that the cave exit, and the open sea, lay behind him. He began to turn the craft round, when something heavy thudded on to the back of the submersible. Then another weight followed, and another.

Now someone was clambering along the craft's deck and trying to get inside the tower. Dakkar pushed the lever to *Full Ahead*. For a second the craft eased sluggishly towards the cave exit, but its speed gathered and Dakkar was rewarded with the sound of someone slipping over and falling heavily on to the rear deck.

Daylight shone across the *Nautilus*'s front deck.

'We've reached open sea, Oginski,' Dakkar said, preparing to submerge and shake off his unwelcome passengers.

As he reached for the submerging handle, a rather damp and dishevelled guard landed with a thump in front of the tower's window. His musket was trained directly at Dakkar's face and he yelled something that Dakkar couldn't hear. The man's meaning, however, was crystal clear. If Dakkar didn't stop, the guard would fire, drowning Dakkar in a storm of glass and shot.

CHAPTER FOUR
TOO MANY SHARKS

For a moment, Dakkar sat motionless in the captain's chair. The thick glass of the porthole muffled the guard's shouts but Dakkar didn't need to hear him to know what he wanted.

The powder in his gun is very likely wet, Dakkar thought, raising his hands to indicate that he wasn't going to try anything, *but is that a gamble I'm willing to take?*

The sound of more feet scrabbling above his head told Dakkar that guards had clambered back on to the tower of the *Nautilus*. His heart thumped. *I can't let them get the sub,* he thought.

Suddenly Dakkar heard faint yells from above and the guard on the front deck glanced back and forth, scanning the water for something. A scream replaced the shouts and the *Nautilus* rolled, tipping Dakkar from his seat. Dakkar caught a glimpse of the guard at the window as he slid from the deck of the *Nautilus*.

'What was that?' Oginski groaned, dragging himself into the captain's place. He looked terrible, his pale skin accentuating the bruise that bloomed on his forehead. Blood stained the shoulder of his white shirt, and his breath rattled as he sat slumped in the seat.

'I don't know,' Dakkar said, peering out of the window. The guard had vanished from the front deck and the hammering at the tower hatch had ceased.

'We should submerge,' Oginski said as he turned the brass ballast wheel handle to fill the sub's hollow hull with water. Dakkar hurried to help him but Oginski shook him off, wincing with each turn.

Slowly, the water rose above the portholes of the *Nautilus* and Dakkar caught his breath. They sank through a mist of red blood. Whatever had rolled the submarine had ditched the other guards into the open sea. Dakkar could see three of them lashing at the water as their heavy uniforms weighed them down. They floated a few feet below the surface.

'Oginski, we must save them!' Dakkar said, pressing his face against the glass. A shadow fell across the porthole, making Dakkar pull back. Something huge had passed above them.

'What is it?' Oginski asked, leaning heavily on the wheel and peering into the murky waters.

'I'm not sure,' Dakkar whispered. 'A fish but it was big! Or maybe even a whale.'

The men outside had seen it too and were thrashing about in the water even more desperately.

The *Nautilus* pitched again as something grazed along her hull. Dakkar gasped as the nose and then the fin and then the tail of an enormous shark glided past the porthole towards the men.

'That's no ordinary shark,' Dakkar gasped. 'It's massive! It must be at least fifty feet long.'

'Too big for . . . a white shark . . .' Oginski said, gritting his teeth. The stain on his shirt had spread. 'We must leave.'

'But those men . . .' Dakkar began.

As he glanced back, he saw the shark open its enormous jaws. Two men could have stood, one on the other's shoulders, and still not spanned the creature's mouth. It swept a poor guard up in one bite, leaving a faint, crimson trail.

Dakkar craned his neck to see the other two men and his eyes widened. Another shark, as big as the first, cruised lazily through the smoky haze of blood that filled the water. Dakkar screwed his eyes shut for a moment. *There was nothing we could do to save them*, he thought, but a pang of regret still nagged at him. He opened his eyes again. The shark had angled slightly and was now heading straight for the *Nautilus*.

'It's coming this way,' Dakkar yelled as the huge jaw opened and the fish hurtled towards them. 'Keep our course!'

Dakkar hurried from the tower down to the front of the *Nautilus*. He scrabbled at the boxes that lay in the front of the submarine and pulled out what looked like a long spear with flights at one end and a ball at the other. A Sea

Arrow, an explosive missile invented by Fulton. Dakkar slipped it into the chamber in the wall of the craft and then pulled back the handle, loading the spring that fired the bomb.

'Oginski, should I fire?' he shouted.

No reply came back.

Cursing, Dakkar bit his lip. There was no time to lose; the shark would hit the *Nautilus* at any moment. He stabbed the firing button with his thumb and was rewarded with a comic *boing* sound as the missile flew from the sub.

Scrambling back to the tower, Dakkar just saw the arrow disappear into the creature's gullet. Its red maw closed on the arrow and then the sea boiled with the explosion. A blood-red fog filled the water and chunks of shark thumped heavily against the *Nautilus* as she rolled and bucked, throwing Dakkar around the tower room like a drunkard in a storm. Oginski slid from his seat and, too weak to hold on, rolled at Dakkar's feet.

Dakkar scrabbled over Oginski into the seat as the *Nautilus* plummeted down into the darkness of the sea, spiralling like a bird diving for a fish. Her planks groaned as Dakkar wrestled with the wheel.

Something banged against the rear of the craft and the world spun around as the *Nautilus* whirled nose over tail. Dakkar clung to the wheel, and Oginski's limp body thumped against the walls, floor and ceiling as each took the place of the other. Maps, spanners, rope and anything that wasn't tied down flew around the cabin, bouncing off

Dakkar's head. Then, in the distance, he saw the ominous outline of a shark growing ever larger.

With a yell, Dakkar wrenched the ballast wheel and blew the ballast tanks, sending water bubbling around them. His head pounded as the *Nautilus* rose upward, righting herself as she went. The shark tracked the submarine's path with ease. Its red mouth, lined with dagger teeth, widened as it scraped past the sub's hull, sending her juddering to port.

'See how you like this,' Dakkar hissed. He reached up to the wall and turned a crank handle rapidly clockwise, panting as he did so. 'Eighteen, nineteen, twenty . . .'

The shark circled back round and Dakkar realised that it was trying to get behind the sub to bite into the rudders of the *Nautilus*. *If that happens, we'll be set adrift, helpless*, he thought, wheeling the craft round to face the oncoming creature once more.

The *Nautilus* shook again and Dakkar shuddered at the sight of the raw gums, serrated teeth and the cold, black button eyes of the shark. He pushed the red button next to the crank handle.

Thousands of volts of electricity pulsed blue around the sub and Dakkar watched as the shark thrashed and writhed in the storm he'd created. The charge died and, still twitching, the shark drifted to the depths below. Dakkar pressed his head against the glass and watched it vanish into the darkness.

'Oginski!' Dakkar yelled, spinning round and dropping down to the prone figure of his mentor on the floor.

Blood pooled from the count's shoulder and he looked paler than before, if that were possible. Dakkar lifted Oginski's shoulders up but his head lolled back. He'd stopped breathing. Dakkar shook Oginski but the big man appeared lifeless. He patted Oginski's face, struggling to remember what he'd been taught about resuscitating those who had stopped breathing. Oginski had taught him a lot as they sat by the sea after their swimming sessions back home in Cornwall. In fact, Dakkar recalled one day when Oginski had timed how long Dakkar could stay underwater – Dakkar had nearly drowned. Remembering what Oginski had done then, Dakkar pulled his mentor's arms up above his head and brought them down again rapidly.

Again, he pumped Oginski's arms. Nothing.

He pressed an ear to Oginski's chest, not noticing the blood that smeared his own cheek. *No heartbeat!*

Dakkar felt numb. Oginski was dead.

CHAPTER FIVE
LIFE OR DEATH?

Dakkar stared at the lifeless form of his mentor. Tears stung his eyes and he stifled a sob. *How can he be dead?* Dakkar thought. *It can't happen.*

'I won't let it happen,' Dakkar snarled, grabbing Oginski's body and dragging it down to the lower cabin of the *Nautilus*.

The man weighed heavy in Dakkar's arms and exhaustion made Dakkar weak. He winced every time Oginski's head accidentally bumped against the walls of the sub or on a step. As he struggled, he remembered an experiment Oginski had once shown him. An experiment first carried out by an Italian called Galvani. He had made a frog's leg twitch with life by passing an electric current through it.

'Galvani believed that animals' muscles have electricity coursing through them,' Oginski had said. 'He may be right. I have conducted many experiments on animal tissue. I even set a pig's heart beating for the briefest amount of time. If it's true then, with a strong enough charge, could we not start a dead man's heart?'

'Oginski, that is monstrous,' Dakkar had objected. 'One must respect the dead. Experiment with human bodies? It doesn't bear thinking about.'

'Don't worry, my prince.' Oginski had laughed. 'I'm not about to go skulking around graveyards at night, looking for fresh corpses. It's just a theory . . .'

Dakkar banged his head on the doorway to the engine room at the rear of the *Nautilus*, snapping himself back to the present. The engine room hummed with power and Dakkar's hair lifted from his scalp as he entered. A blue light filled this chamber even though the Voltalith lay housed in a round flat case in the centre of the engine. Under Oginski's tuition, Dakkar was beginning to understand the function of each of these machine parts, but at the moment it looked like a confusing bird's nest of wire, cogs and levers all ticking and buzzing with energy. Two thick tubes coiled from the case that held the Voltalith. This was how Oginski harnessed the power of the electric rock somehow; it flowed through copper wire wrapped in thick Indian rubber.

'If I can use the power of the Voltalith . . .' Dakkar murmured, slipping on thick rubber gauntlets. Oginski insisted that they wore these whenever they handled the engine parts. Dakkar had already witnessed the destructive power of the Voltalith and the protective qualities of the gauntlets.

Dakkar disconnected the two thick rubber hoses from the flywheel of the engine. The whine of the *Nautilus*'s engine slowly died and Dakkar felt his stomach lurch as the submarine stopped her forward motion and began a slow downward arc.

Electricity from the Voltalith spat and crackled at the ends of each cable. A blinding blue light bathed the whole room, and even through the thick gauntlets Dakkar could feel his knuckles and joints beginning to stiffen and fizz with the charge.

For a second, Dakkar hesitated. *What if it doesn't work? What if Oginski isn't truly dead and this kills him?* He took one last look at the white face, made all the more deathly by the livid bruise and the red blood.

Uttering a silent prayer, Dakkar plunged the cable into Oginski's chest. Sparks leapt and danced around the two of them as Oginski's whole body arched and shook. His face tightened into a rictus grin. Every muscle in Oginski's body knotted and Dakkar heard a long, rattling breath.

He pulled back, stumbling against the engine as Oginski's body shook, flopping on the floor like a landed fish. Then he lay still.

Dakkar leaned against the engine, the two cables still humming in his fists. *I've failed*, he thought as hot tears welled from his eyes and a deep, wracking sob forced its way up from his stomach.

Oginski gave an enormous gasp and his eyes flew open. Dakkar leapt in surprise, nearly dropping the cables. The big man fell back on the floor, panting for breath.

'Dakkar?' he said, his voice feeble and cracked. 'What happened?'

'Oginski! You're alive!' Dakkar threw himself down next to his mentor and hugged him awkwardly, trying not to touch him with the cables.

Oginski groaned. 'Of course I am,' he said, wincing. 'Are . . . we safe?'

'We are. Let's get you to a bunk,' Dakkar replied.

He hastily reconnected the thick cables and then helped Oginski to his feet. Oginski shuffled through the sub, wincing as he went. At one point he stopped, retching blood and falling heavily against the walls of the *Nautilus*. Finally, he collapsed on to the small pallet bed in his tiny cabin.

'I'll get the *Nautilus* to the surface and then we need to find you a doctor,' Dakkar said, easing Oginski's head on to a pillow.

The journey back to England took Dakkar several days longer than he expected. On the voyage out to Elba, they had taken turns to captain the *Nautilus*, allowing each other to rest. With Oginski unconscious below, Dakkar was now the only crew member and had to do everything himself. Despite his best efforts at dressing the wound on Oginski's shoulder, it grew hot and gave off a horrible smell. He became feverish and would drift in and out of consciousness, shouting deliriously sometimes, crying for help at others. Each time Dakkar had to surface and hurry to Oginski's cabin.

'Don't worry,' Dakkar reassured him, wiping his brow with a damp cloth. 'We'll soon have you back in the castle.' The castle was the name given to their home, a tower house that stood alone on a bleak, Cornish cliff.

'No!' Oginski said, grabbing Dakkar's sleeve. 'Doctor Walbridge. He's the only one I trust . . .'

'But what about Doctor Ives? He lives close to the castle,' Dakkar said, easing Oginski back on to his pillow.

'I know Walbridge of old,' Oginski said, his breathing heavy. 'I can trust him. Ives is a gossip and a quack!'

'Very well,' Dakkar said, keeping his voice soft and soothing. 'Where can I find this Doctor Walbridge?'

'Lyme Regis,' Oginski replied, his voice becoming drowsy as the effort of speaking became too much. 'Go to Cutter's Cove, just west of Lyme . . .' The big man's eyelids drooped and soon his snores filled the tiny cabin.

Dakkar sighed and shook his head as he returned to the helm. He slumped into the captain's seat. He had only snatched a few hours of sleep since they'd escaped from the island of Elba. The stretch of the Mediterranean Sea they approached now was cluttered with naval vessels from all over the world, not to mention pirates from the coast of Africa.

To add to Dakkar's worries, the stresses of their Elba adventure were beginning to show on the *Nautilus*. Water seeped gently through the planks in a number of places where musket balls had lodged in the wood and the engine made a strange clattering sound. Dakkar didn't dare submerge too deep as the pressure drove water in at a faster rate. An inch of seawater sloshed around the floors already. Dakkar's attempts at bailing some out proved successful but as he sailed on his work was quickly undone.

But if I'm to get through the Strait of Gibraltar, I'll have to submerge, he thought, biting his lip. The strait was the entrance to the Mediterranean Sea, an eight-mile-wide channel of sea between Africa and the Rock of Gibraltar, which bristled with British warships and cannon.

Dakkar sailed on, travelling at night and trying to rest during the day. He stopped regularly to check on the ailing Oginski.

'Remember, Dakkar,' Oginski croaked, 'sail deep out of the strait . . . The Mediterranean flows out into the Atlantic . . .'

'I know, Oginski, I will, I promise,' Dakkar said, giving his mentor a sip of water.

Oginski had explained to Dakkar before they'd set off for Elba that the waters of the Mediterranean were more salty and dense than those of the Atlantic. As a result, the waters of the Mediterranean sank to a greater depth and flowed out into the Atlantic while the Atlantic waters flowed into the Mediterranean above them.

As they neared Gibraltar, Dakkar saw more and more ships. He kept as far from other vessels as possible and submerged only when he had to. He saw American flags, Portuguese, French and British. In the far distance, black outlines cruised the horizon and Dakkar wondered if they were Barbary pirates, searching for victims to attack and plunder, selling their captives as slaves in far off Timbuktu.

Finally, he was forced to stay submerged and tried to ignore the steady trickling noise that told him the sea was coming in. The huge silhouettes of warships and merchant vessels blocked out the weak sunshine that struggled to penetrate the water. Dakkar gritted his teeth and sank the *Nautilus* even deeper.

He felt the current of the Mediterranean push the sub out towards the open ocean and switched the engine to full power. Stumbling a little at the sudden lurch forward, Dakkar managed a grin at the speed at which they now travelled. It grew warmer in the cramped cabins and Dakkar stared out through the portholes, watching fish skim by, listening to the water bubble against the hull of the submarine.

Soon they were in Atlantic waters. Oginski cried out again, forcing Dakkar to stop the *Nautilus* and hurry down to his mentor's cabin. The count sat up in his bed, blankets scrunched around his lower half, sweat dripping from his forehead. He gripped Dakkar's arm, making him wince. His hand felt clammy and cold.

'Cutter's Cove, Dakkar,' Oginski hissed, shaking. 'The men there will help me . . . they are loyal to me . . . Don't be afraid . . .'

'Oginski, you're exhausting yourself,' Dakkar said, trying to pull his wrist free. 'Don't worry – I've fought off pirates, remember?' He smiled at the sweet memory of blowing up Captain Jean Lafitte's cabin in a Louisiana swamp.

'Worse than pirates,' Oginski gasped, his eyes wide. 'Be careful!'

He fell back into a rambling, delirious sleep, leaving Dakkar to wonder what could be worse than pirates.

CHAPTER SIX
CUTTER'S COVE

The *Nautilus* bounced and skipped over the waves, making Dakkar's stomach leap and lurch. After more than a week of stolen sleep, bailing the *Nautilus* and patching up the worsening leaks, his head pounded and his eyelids felt like lead.

Oginski murmured and muttered in his sleep. He took water and a little bread mushed into porridge but didn't fully wake.

Dakkar slumped on the wheel of the *Nautilus*, nodding and startling back to wakefulness. He rubbed his eyes and squinted through the porthole at the grey line on the horizon.

'England,' he whispered. Then he jumped out of his seat. 'England! Oginski we've made it!'

Dakkar leapt around the cabin, laughing and cheering. Then he stopped. Oginski couldn't reply. *Even if I get him to Cutter's Cove, will he make it?* Dakkar thought.

He hurried down to the cabin, where Oginski lay huddled in the screwed-up blankets. The smell of infection and stale sweat made Dakkar's stomach churn but he crouched beside him.

'We're nearly there,' he whispered. 'I won't let you die.'

Ships plied the sea nearby as Dakkar approached Cutter's Cove and he took a huge risk in not submerging. *If I submerged again*, he thought, kicking at the water that played around his ankles, *I'm not sure I'd be able to surface again.*

The cove had been drawn in on the chart that Dakkar had found. It clearly wasn't on any of the charts used by the navy or merchant ships. It appeared to be very sheltered, a small inlet carved into steep cliffs. Dakkar shivered at the thought of entering the port so openly. *Who is there? And why isn't this cove marked on the maps?*

The sea battered against the cliffs here and at first Dakkar stared blankly for some indication of the cove's entrance. The *Nautilus* rocked on the waves now they were close to shore and Dakkar had to keep steering her away from the treacherous rocks that jutted from the sea.

As they rounded a headland, he noticed an incredibly narrow gap in the cliff. The water heaved up and down in this channel, which seemed to lead deep inland.

Surely that can't be it, he thought. *We'll be smashed to pieces if we go in.*

But after forty minutes of scouting along the cliffs and dodging sharp rocks, Dakkar resigned himself to the fact that the steep, narrow inlet had to be the entrance to Cutter's Cove.

He turned the *Nautilus* round and steered for the gap in the cliffs. The sub seemed to fly up on the waves' crests and Dakkar could see the rough rock face of the wall pass just a few inches from the hull.

The waves dropped suddenly and Dakkar's stomach flipped as the *Nautilus* plummeted. Outside, he heard rock scraping along the planking. Dakkar screwed his eyes shut and nudged the wheel slightly, bringing her to the middle of the narrow channel.

Once more Dakkar felt the *Nautilus* being lifted and again the cliff edge clunked against her sides. Through the porthole, he could see the end of the channel and a strip of grey sky. A wave suddenly smacked against the front of the craft, sending her to port and the side of the entrance. A huge bang echoed throughout the *Nautilus* and a fine spray of water hissed through the planks close to Dakkar's head.

Dakkar gave a grunt as he wrestled with the wheel and brought the sub back under control before she could scrape the full length of the cliff. The *Nautilus* gave a shudder and then leapt into the air as she bounced over another wave.

The walls of the sea channel vanished behind Dakkar and left him staring at a tiny cove. It made him think of a huge sea cave whose ceiling had collapsed, leaving a deep hole. He could see now how the cliffs rose to meet the sea, forming a wall at the front of the cove, and behind it how the land sloped away from the cliffs. The sides of the cove were steep and a few stone cottages and sheds clung to them, looking as if they could fall into the water at any moment. Here and there, Dakkar could see caves punched into the cliff face. A long stone jetty reached out into the sea, which surged and swirled in and out. It was early March but grey winter clouds still hung above him, making every-thing dull and lifeless.

Dakkar steered for the jetty, where a small group of men had gathered with ropes and grappling irons to bring the *Nautilus* in. They carried rifles too, Dakkar noticed. For a moment, he wanted to turn and flee. These men had seen too much and Oginski had said they were worse than pirates. Dakkar's heart thumped.

As he approached the jetty, Dakkar flinched as the first hook thumped on to the top of the *Nautilus*, then another. Dakkar felt the sideways pull as the men brought her alongside the jetty. He shut the engine down and clam-bered up the ladder. The thud of boots told him that the men were clambering on board to meet him.

Dakkar threw open the hatch at the top of the tower and found a rifle pointing at him once again. He froze and felt the blood drain from his face.

Three men perched round the edge of the tower. They were tall and strongly built like Oginski, with stern, scarred and weather-beaten faces. Two wore moustaches waxed to a point at the ends while the other sported a thick beard. They reminded Dakkar of Napoleon's Imperial Guard.

But what made Dakkar freeze in fear was the emblem on each of their black uniforms. A large letter C, a trident and a snake. The symbol for Cryptos.

CHAPTER SEVEN

WARRIORS FROM THE PAST

One of the men stood taller than the rest. His bald head and thick beard distinguished him from the others, who wore berets and moustaches. He stared down at Dakkar, his lip curling.

'Keep that rifle trained on him, Serge,' the man said. 'If the boy so much as blinks, blow his head off. Bolton, get inside that boat, see if anyone else is lurking down there.'

'Aye, Cutter,' said another of the men, a pistol ready in his fist. He clambered past Dakkar and down through the hatch.

This can't be! Dakkar looked from Cutter to the rifle pointed at him. *What shall I do? Where are the men who are meant to be loyal to Oginski?*

'Please, you've got to help me,' Dakkar said, clenching his fists then freezing as the rifle barrel twitched.

'You've come to the wrong place for help, my

friend,' said Cutter, his laugh echoed by the men around him.

'My mentor, Count Oginski, he lies below on the brink of death,' Dakkar pleaded. 'He told me to come here. He needs a doctor.'

The mention of Oginski turned Cutter's face pale. Serge lowered the rifle for a second and then brought it up again. A mutter of consternation rippled among the men who had crowded around.

'Cutter!' Bolton called from the tower. 'Come quickly!'

Cutter lunged towards Dakkar, making the boy flinch, but the big man barged past him and clambered down into the *Nautilus*. Dakkar made to follow him but Serge edged forward and jabbed the rifle barrel against his cheek.

'Don't move until Cutter says you can,' Serge hissed, and eased back a little.

A moment later, Cutter's huge form emerged from the hatch with Oginski over his shoulder. Dakkar realised just how much Oginski had wasted away during the voyage. Cutter was a big man and obviously strong, but even so he carried Oginski out of the hatch easily.

'Is he alive, Cutter?' Serge asked, taking his eyes from Dakkar.

'Barely,' Cutter said, his face grim. 'We need to get him to Walbridge as quickly as possible. Piper, ready a carriage. Serge, bring that boy to the cottage. He has some questions to answer.'

A small man scurried off ahead of them towards the cottages and Cutter climbed down off the *Nautilus* with Oginski still over his shoulder. Serge glowered at Dakkar from under bushy eyebrows and flicked the rifle to the left, indicating that Dakkar should step on to the stone jetty and follow Cutter. Dakkar eased himself down and stumbled towards the huddle of cottages. The men walked alongside him in silence and, every now and then, Serge would jab Dakkar in the back with the gun barrel.

Seagulls screamed and wheeled around the rock face that rose above them. At the end of the jetty, Dakkar could see a cobbled quay with the small cottages and storehouses made of neat grey stone. Behind them a path wound up to the cliff top.

Oginski groaned feebly, his arms swinging loose. Tears stung Dakkar's eyes at the sight of the great man brought so low. Cutter pushed a cottage door open and disappeared inside. Dakkar followed, despite everything, enjoying the warmth that washed over him.

The door led into the cottage's kitchen and living area. Clean, scrubbed tables stood in regimented rows on a stone floor off which you could eat it was so well scrubbed. Everything about the room barked discipline and organisation to Dakkar. Jars and bottles stood to attention on the shelves in neat rows. Maps and charts covered the walls.

Cutter swept away the plates and cutlery set out on one of the tables nearest the fire that blazed in the hearth. He lay Oginski down gently, cradling his head. The men crowded round, pulling their caps off.

'Will he be all right, Cutter?' asked one of the men, his eyes wide.

'He looks so pale,' another added, shaking his head.

Dakkar watched in disbelief as yet another wiped a tear from his eye.

'We'll see,' Cutter said, and tore at Oginski's filthy shirt. 'Get warm water and fresh clothes. Jackson, clean and dress that wound as best as you can. It will soon be dark and we'll travel to Lyme then.'

Cutter turned to Dakkar and pointed to a table in the corner of the room. Dakkar followed him and sat down on a wooden stool.

'So you are the illustrious Prince Dakkar,' Cutter said, folding his arms and sitting back in the chair opposite Dakkar. 'The one our leader hopes will save the civilised nations from Cryptos.'

'I don't know what you mean,' Dakkar muttered, feeling his face grow warm. 'Oginski isn't your leader!'

A shadow passed over Cutter's square face. 'He was once,' he said. 'And he will be again.'

Another of the men brought two bowls of steaming broth and some chunks of bread. Dakkar's mouth watered. The smell was so good after days of stale biscuit and salt beef. Cutter waved a hand to the bowl and Dakkar couldn't resist snatching a spoon and slurping up the soup. *This is all wrong*, he thought. *Oginski is dying on that table and here I am eating with this agent of Cryptos.* He put his spoon down.

'I just want Oginski to live,' Dakkar said, narrowing his eyes at Cutter.

'Eat your soup – you'll need your strength for the journey to Lyme,' Cutter said, waving a dismissive hand. 'As for Oginski, we'll do our best.'

Dakkar picked up the spoon again. Oginski had talked a little about his past but not gone into details. Dakkar didn't know that his mentor had once commanded men and guards as Count Cryptos did. Had Oginski once called himself Count Cryptos? Had he ever plotted to overthrow countries or even empires?

'You served with Oginski?' Dakkar said, his voice thick with the soup.

Cutter rested his elbow on the table and pushed his shoulder forward so that the Cryptos insignia on the top of his arm faced Dakkar. 'Cryptos Red Faction,' he said, pointing to the insignia. 'We were Oginski's most loyal men, his elite fighters. Our missions took us all over the world. Twenty men now guard this cove for him. Over the years, Franciszek Oginski saved the lives of every one of us. We swore an oath of loyalty to him.'

'Then why do you still wear the badge of Count Cryptos?' Dakkar said, frowning.

'Cryptos is more than just one man. It is an army,' Cutter replied, raising his eyebrows as if surprised by the question. 'We are loyal to our comrades too. When Franciszek Oginski turned against his brothers, we swore we would never harm him but we couldn't turn against our other comrades. It was a dark day.'

'So you don't fight for anyone now?' Dakkar said.

'We will help our brothers, if they call,' Cutter said.

'But not if it involves Franciszek Oginski. In the meantime we keep busy – a little smuggling, some robbery. We
wait for him to return and lead us once more.'

Dakkar sat speechless. *I can't imagine Oginski leading these
men*, he thought. *Surely he wasn't like the Count Cryptos I
knew – ruthless and cold.*

The cottage door burst open and the man called Piper
stood there, panting. He looked as if the devil himself
were after him.

'The carriage is ready, Cutter,' he panted. 'The men are
ready with a stretcher to carry the count up the cliff path.'

'Good work, Piper,' Cutter growled, rising to his feet.
'Oginski would be impressed with your speed.'

Piper gave a tight smile and nodded.

These men really do care about Oginski, Dakkar thought.
Why didn't he try to reform them?

Dakkar watched, forgotten by the men as they hurried
to lift Oginski on to the stretcher. Four held the stretcher
by the handles, two at the front and two at the back, each
flanked by a man armed with a rifle. They eased their
burden out through the door and into the darkening night.

Cutter nodded to Dakkar to follow them. The big man
grabbed a thick woollen jacket that hung on the back of
the door and threw it to Dakkar.

'That'll keep you from perishing in the cold,' he said.
'Now, come with us.'

Darkness filled the quay and some of the men carried
lanterns that swung as they moved, making the cobbles
dance. Dakkar felt a little dizzy.

He glanced back at the black outline of the *Nautilus*, bobbing at the end of the jetty, and bit his lip.

'Don't worry,' Cutter called back to him. 'The rest of the men will guard Oginski's sub with their lives.'

Dakkar hurried next to Oginski's stretcher as the men began to march along the narrow quay. As they moved, Dakkar noticed crumbling, derelict fishermen's cottages skirting the cobbled space. He shuddered. Had the people here moved out of their own free will?

'This place was long abandoned when we took it over,' said the man holding the back of the stretcher, as if reading Dakkar's mind. 'The entrance to the cove collapsed, making it almost impossible to get boats out to sea. The villagers left for easier ports.'

Soon, the path rose steeply and turned into steps carved out of the crumbling rock. The men's pace didn't change and Dakkar found himself panting for breath as the weeks of deprivation and effort caught up with him. The soup he had eaten earlier threatened to force its way out of his stomach and his head thumped. He glanced up as the men's feet pounded in a uniform rhythm on the steps. Oginski's stretcher remained level, and even though the men at the back were virtually holding the big man above their heads their faces betrayed no sign of effort.

Soon they crested the cliff and climbed on to a narrow, muddy track that led into the darkness. The cliff path whirled and veered in front of him. He felt his legs give way at the knee and he pitched forward, bumping into one of the guards. Suddenly he found himself staring back down on to the cottages, tiny now they had climbed to the top of the cliff. He stumbled straight towards the edge of the path and the drop below. He couldn't stop himself. He was falling.

CHAPTER EIGHT
NIGHT ATTACK

Dakkar felt weightless for a second. He tried to scream but his dry mouth and throat let out a hoarse croak.

Then a firm hand yanked at his collar, choking him and dragging him back. His feet kicked forward and he fell hard on to his backside. Cutter stood over him, his hands on his hips.

'Careful, lad,' he said. 'It's a long way down.'

'Thank you,' Dakkar gasped, his voice like sandpaper.

He felt strong hands sweep him up and half push, half drag him up the path towards a waiting carriage. As he came closer, he could see that it was quite plain – more a box on wheels with a door at each side and thick curtains covering the open windows.

'Get the boy inside,' Cutter barked.

The carriage door creaked open and Dakkar was dragged up. He eased himself on to a bench at the back, glad to have the chance to sit and rest. A moment later,

Oginski was pushed in on his stretcher. The whiteness of his face stood out in the darkness. Dakkar rested a palm on the man's clammy brow.

'Don't you dare die, Oginski,' he whispered, tears prickling his eyes. 'Don't you dare!'

Piper climbed in and sat next to Dakkar.

'Do not worry, my friend,' he said, laying a hand on Dakkar's arm. 'We will get him to Doctor Walbridge. Oginski is strong. He has cheated death before.'

Serge, the man who had held Dakkar at gunpoint, climbed in and sat on the other side of him. The carriage began to rock as the driver smacked the reins, waking the horses into motion.

'How did he come to be so badly hurt?' Serge said, looking down on his fallen leader and shaking his head.

'There was an explosion,' Dakkar muttered, looking at the floor. 'And some men shot at us. A bullet caught Oginski's shoulder.'

'You've been at sea for some days,' Piper said, looking keenly at Dakkar. 'Where did this happen?'

Weariness ate at Dakkar's very bones. He didn't have the energy to think and didn't want to say. But, looking down at Oginski's frail form, it all seemed so pointless. He heaved a sigh.

'We were on Elba,' he said, grinding the heel of his hand into his eye. 'Trying to stop Cryptos from killing Napoleon.'

'Just you and Franciszek?' Serge said, his eyes wide.

'How many men did Cryptos have?'

'Which of Franciszek's brothers was against you?' Piper asked, leaning forward.

'I don't know,' Dakkar admitted. 'They had some kind of beast but it fled when an imperial guard shot at it.'

'So you didn't see any Cryptos guards?' Serge frowned.

'No,' Dakkar said slowly. 'Only some badges that Bonaparte's guards said they had taken from Cryptos's.'

'Sounds like you've been led on a wild goose chase,' Piper said.

'A what?' Dakkar said.

'A pointless mission,' Serge explained. 'If Cryptos really wanted Bonaparte dead, he would be. They wanted to draw Oginski out, distract him, maybe from a larger plan.'

'But Oginski had reliable information that Cryptos was going to kill Bonaparte,' Dakkar said.

'We heard that rumour too,' Piper said. 'Not that we'd have done much about it.'

'I did wonder why he was so keen to protect such a man as Bonaparte, Dakkar said, stamping his foot. 'He has caused nothing but misery in Europe. He's worse than Cryptos himself!'

'That's one point of view.' Serge nodded in agreement. 'Oginski admires him, though. He'd often point out that even during his short time on Elba, he has established democratic councils and improved the irrigation and drainage systems for the people. Anyway, if Cryptos wants Bonaparte dead, Oginski wants him alive!'

'It's true,' Piper said.

'Quiet in there,' hissed Cutter, banging on the side of the carriage. 'We have company.'

'Soldiers,' Piper whispered, staring out of the carriage. 'On the lookout for smugglers, no doubt.'

'Stop!' shouted a gruff voice from outside. The carriage rumbled to a halt. Dakkar's heart pounded. Piper clicked back the hammer on his pistol. 'What's your business, travelling at this time of night?'

'We have a poor unfortunate who needs a doctor,' Cutter called back. Dakkar peered out of the window door into the night.

'If we don't get him to Lyme, he'll surely die.' He could see at least ten soldiers, the colour of their uniforms bleached blue by the moonlight. They blocked the narrow lane, their rifles cocked and trained on Cutter.

Where are the other men who have been running alongside the carriage? Dakkar thought. There had been at least six of them, but now the big man stood alone.

'We'll need to search your carriage,' said the officer in charge of the soldiers as they inched forward, rifles levelled at Cutter.

'Sorry, boys,' Cutter said, raising his hands, 'but we're in a hurry and can't be waiting.'

A shot rang out from the lane and one of the soldiers fell to the ground with a scream. Dakkar threw himself back into the carriage as more gunfire lit up the lane. The soldiers' rifles roared, sending bullets ripping through the top of the carriage. Then Dakkar heard the grunts and yells of hand-to-hand combat. He looked out again, expecting to see a bloodbath. Instead, he saw Cutter swinging his heavy fist into the officer's chin. The blow lifted the soldier off the ground and into the hedgerow that lined the lane.

Cutter's men had crept round the side of the soldiers and leapt from the bushes, taking them by surprise. The guns had gone off in all directions, missing Cutter. Dakkar saw Bolton crack a soldier on the top of the head with his fist, sending the man crumpling to the earth, unconscious. Another of Cutter's men lifted a soldier above his head and threw him to the ground.

Soon, all the soldiers were strewn across the lane. One held his arm where the first shot had winged him.

'Tie them up quickly,' Cutter said, clicking his fingers. 'We don't have time to waste.' He glanced round at Dakkar. 'Don't worry, your highness – they're all alive. If we killed one of them then the place would be crawling with His Majesty's army. As it is, these boys will probably be too embarrassed to report this little episode.'

Dakkar nodded, sliding back on to his bench. Oginski groaned as the carriage began to rattle along the lane again.

The rest of the journey proved uneventful and Dakkar tried to stay awake, keeping watch over the limp figure on the stretcher at his feet, but exhaustion overwhelmed him. He dozed fitfully, being shaken awake every now and then by the ruts and potholes in the lane that made the carriage jump and lurch. Time seemed disjointed, stopping and starting until Dakkar didn't have a clue how long they had travelled for.

'Wake up, boy. We're here!' Serge said, poking Dakkar in the arm.

Dakkar forced his heavy eyes open to see the men sliding Oginski's stretcher out of the carriage.

They stood in a cobbled street that plunged steeply down towards the sea, which hushed and shushed them somewhere behind the claustrophobic press of little houses. The men, led by Cutter, hurried across the street to a two-floor stone cottage. Dakkar could see its occupants were a little more well-to-do than their neighbours by the freshly painted door and the brass knocker.

Cutter ignored the knocker and hammered on the door with his fist. Dakkar glanced around the street, expecting lights to flare in the tiny windows that looked out darkly at them. Cutter thumped at the door again.

A square panel opened in the door and a rifle barrel poked out.

'Who is it?' hissed a voice from inside. 'And what d'you mean, coming here, banging on my door in the middle of the night?'

'It's Cutter, Doctor Walbridge,' the big man replied in a low but urgent voice. 'I have a patient on the verge of death.'

The barrel vanished back through the panel and Dakkar heard bolts being drawn back. The door opened to reveal a portly gentleman in a long nightshirt and a cap on his round head. Grey frizzes of hair poked wildly from under the nightcap and he glared at them all over a pair of half-moon glasses.

'Get inside,' he snapped. 'You'll wake the whole town with your bellowing and stamping around.'

They all followed Cutter and the stretcher as they squeezed into the narrow hallway. Ten men and Oginski on the stretcher filled the house and spilled into the tiny living room that adjoined the hall.

'You men wait here,' Walbridge said, waving vaguely at the rooms. 'Take the patient upstairs.'

Dakkar went to follow Walbridge and Cutter but the doctor turned and raised a hand to stop him.

'Let him come, doctor,' Cutter said. 'He brought Oginski to us.'

'Oginski!' Walbridge exclaimed, pushing his glasses up his nose and staring over the shoulders of the stretcher bearers. 'My word. I would never have recognised him. Quickly – get him up to the room on the left.'

They hurried up the cramped stairs and Dakkar stood forgotten as the doctor hurried to get Oginski on to a bed.

'Breathing shallow but regular,' Walbridge muttered, pressing an ear to his chest. 'Heartbeat fast.'

'He took a rifle ball in the shoulder,' Dakkar said.

Walbridge paused and stared at Dakkar over his glasses. 'I can see that, young man,' the doctor said. 'I am just assessing whether or not Count Oginski is strong enough for me to remove it.'

Dakkar watched helplessly as the doctor undressed

Oginski and examined his wasted body. Finally, Walbridge shook his head.

'Is he going to be all right?' Dakkar asked, feeling the blood drain from his face.

'He is very weak,' Walbridge asked. 'He has internal injuries and the wound is infected. There's nothing for it but to remove the shot from his shoulder.'

'His life hangs in the balance then?' Cutter said, with a catch in his throat.

Walbridge nodded. 'I will do my very best,' he said, his voice softening. 'Oginski is an old friend of mine. Now you must leave me to do my work.'

CHAPTER NINE
THE OLD OGINSKI

Dakkar followed Cutter downstairs to await the results of Walbridge's operation. He felt numb and cold.

They stepped into the tiny living room. A table had been pushed back and men sat on the floor or on the few chairs that stood there. A small fire smouldered in the grate and Piper knelt, trying to add kindling to bring it back to life. Not that a fire was needed; the crush of the men filled the room with warmth. Dakkar sat by the window and listened as they talked about past adventures with Oginski.

'Do you remember the time we blew that ammunition store in Seville?' Serge said, grinning. 'Franciszek nearly went up with it himself. Had to run back for Bolton.'

'I'd been shot in the ankle,' Bolton protested, then he gave a sad smile. 'But, yes, he came back for me.'

'He wouldn't have abandoned any of us,' Cutter said. 'He pulled me from that sinking ship. We both nearly drowned.'

Dakkar felt jealous that these men shared a past with Oginski, time Dakkar knew nothing about.

'Different now, though, isn't it?' Piper stood up and stared into the fire. 'Now he's got his tame little prince.'

Dakkar looked up. The eyes of every man in the room were on him. Eyes full of menace.

'What do you mean?' Dakkar said, his voice barely audible.

'We'd never have let 'im get so close to death,' Serge muttered, scowling at Dakkar. 'If you weren't around, maybe he'd have come back to us.'

'Oginski left us long before this pipsqueak turned up,' Cutter said, spitting into the fire. 'You can't blame Dakkar. But what days, eh?'

'I can't believe Oginski would commit . . . crimes,' Dakkar said, his voice faltering. The Count Cryptos he'd met killed without a moment's thought and plotted world domination. 'Oginski isn't like that.'

'More's the pity,' Piper muttered, looking darkly at Dakkar. 'But believe us when we say that there was a time when Franciszek would have taken life and liberty from anyone who stood in his way.'

The night dragged on. The men took it in turns to sleep or to keep watch out of the window.

'Those military men won't get back to their barracks until late morning but we'll keep our eyes peeled,' Cutter said.

Dakkar dozed, startling to wakefulness whenever

someone spoke or moved. Sometimes he stole out to the bottom of the narrow stairs and looked up at the candle-light flickering from under the door of Oginski's room.

'It's a ticklish business,' Cutter said, ruffling Dakkar's hair. 'You can be a better help by being rested and refreshed in the morning.'

Dawn broke, grey and watery, as Dakkar waited. Someone put a plate of bread and cheese in front of him but he barely ate any of it.

Finally, the heavy tread of the doctor brought Dakkar to his feet, sending the chair he sat on clattering to the floor. He ran out to the stairs and looked up at Walbridge's drawn face. Cutter and the others crowded around him.

'Well?' he said, not daring to meet Walbridge's eyes.

'Oginski survived the removal of the bullet,' Walbridge said, rubbing his eyes. Dakkar noticed the man's bloody apron and sleeves. 'The next few days are crucial. If he can fight the infection, we may be able to save his arm. Otherwise I'll have to amputate, and even then he may not survive.'

'Can I see him?' Dakkar said, starting forward to the stairs.

Walbridge blocked his path. 'The man needs rest,' he said. 'Leave him to sleep. He is safe and secure here. I will keep an eye on him.'

'But –'

'Oginski is as strong as an ox, Dakkar,' Cutter said, gripping him by the shoulders and staring deep into his eyes. 'He is a fighter. You get some rest.'

'How can I rest when Oginski's life hangs in the balance?' Dakkar muttered and stalked out of the cottage, letting the fresh sea breeze slap him awake.

They care about him too, Dakkar thought. His mind was a confusion of fear and even jealousy. *But how can I even talk with these men? They'd go back to Cryptos tomorrow if Oginski led them.*

Dakkar shoved his hand into his pocket and pulled out the claw that he'd found on Elba. He turned it over in his fingers.

Piper leaned against the front door of the cottage, his arms folded.

'That's a mean-looking spike and no mistake,' he said, nodding to the claw. 'Where's it from?'

'Elba,' Dakkar replied. 'I found it wedged in a door from there. I wonder what kind of creature it is.'

'There's someone who might know something,' Piper said, nodding out to sea. 'A girl. Mary Anning's her name.'

'A girl?' Dakkar frowned.

'Yeah,' Piper continued. 'She collects all manner of strange petrified things from the beach and sells 'em to folks. Dragon's Teeth and Devil's Fingernails. That thing's as close to what she sells as I can imagine. She might know what kind of creature it's from.'

'You really think she'll be able to help?' Dakkar asked dubiously.

'Well, if nothing more, it'll get you down on the beach.' Piper grinned. 'There's a stiff breeze coming in from the sea. That'll put some colour in your cheeks at least.' He winked. 'And what's better for taking your mind off poor old Oginski than talkin' to a pretty young girl?'

Dakkar felt his cheeks redden. 'Thank you, Piper,' he muttered and headed to the beach.

The town had woken up now but it was a grey morning in early spring. A few people walked past him, the fishermen touching the brim of their caps, and a few hardy, well-off gentlefolk giving him a cold stare while holding on to their hats.

Dakkar made his way down on to the beach and scraped his feet through the shingle as he strolled along. He took a deep breath and felt the wind whipping his face. The waves pounded the shore just a few feet from him.

He plunged his hands into his pockets. The claw felt sharp and hard in his palm. *Maybe this Anning girl could help*, Dakkar thought, but he strongly suspected that Piper was just trying to divert his thoughts away from poor old Oginski.

A metallic ringing carried on the wind, making Dakkar pause. He glanced up the beach to the cliffs and saw a girl hammering at the rock with what looked like a tiny pick. Her long skirt and shawl flapped in the stiffening breeze and she held on to her bonnet with one hand as she swung the small pick with the other.

Dakkar hurried through the shingle to get nearer.

The girl turned; Dakkar could see a pair of fierce eyes and a tight, buttonhole mouth. Black ringlets of hair spilled out of her bonnet's brim, hardly containing it at all.

'I beg your pardon. I didn't mean to –' Dakkar began, but a rock fell from above him, landing inches away, then another and another.

Small stones bounced off his head and shoulder. Then a deep rumbling followed and shadow fell across the two of them as the cliff collapsed.

CHAPTER TEN
MARY ANNING

The roar of the crumbling cliff filled Dakkar's ears. Dust clouded around them and huge boulders crashed together, cracking and splintering in the chaos. Without hesitating, Dakkar threw himself towards the girl, grabbing her round the waist. They tumbled on to the shingle as earth piled forward, threatening to engulf them. Still holding on to the girl, Dakkar rolled over and over again away down the beach. Soil grimed his eyes and made his mouth feel dry and gritty.

The thundering subsided and, for a second, Dakkar and the girl lay still on the shingle. A mountain of rock and earth lay inches from them. An occasional stone or pebble bounced down, clicking and cracking as it did. The blood pounded in Dakkar's head and he panted for breath. Then, suddenly, the girl was struggling, kicking and slapping at him.

'Let go of me, you scoundrel!' she yelled, scrambling to

her feet. She was a local girl; her accent told Dakkar that much. She glared at Dakkar. Her bonnet was pushed back from her head and dirt smeared her clothes and face. 'What do you mean by leapin' on a defenceless young lady like that? I've a mind to call the constable!'

'I was saving you from the rockfall!' Dakkar said, staring at her as if she were mad. 'You would have been crushed if I hadn't intervened.'

'Crushed?' The girl's eyes widened. 'I've been diggin' in these cliffs all my life. My old dad used to do the same, God rest his soul. I was about to get out of the way but you crept up on me!'

'Crept up?' Dakkar muttered. He gritted his teeth and gave a short bow. 'Well, ma'am, forgive me. It wasn't my intention to alarm you. I thought I was saving your life. Now, if you'll excuse me . . .'

He turned and began to walk away, his feet scrunching on the pebbles.

'Savin' my life? The day Mary Anning needs her life savin',' the girl called after him, 'will be the day she dies!'

'Two things! One: that doesn't make sense,' Dakkar said, stopping and turning round. 'And two: did you just say your name is Mary Anning?'

'Who wants to know?' she said, narrowing her eyes at Dakkar.

'My name is Dakkar. Prince Dakkar of Bundelkhand, to be precise,' he said, giving another short bow. 'I was wondering if you've ever seen anything like this before?'

Dakkar pulled the claw from his pocket and held it in front of Mary.

Mary's face fell. 'I 'aven't seen nothin' like that before,' she snapped, turning and hurrying away. 'I don't care who you are. I don't know anythin' about it!'

Dakkar stood for a second, watching her. He hadn't expected a reaction like that. Then he started after her.

'I think you do, miss,' he called, and stamped through the shingle. 'If you'd just stop and talk to me.'

'Go away!' she shouted, and began to run surprisingly fast considering her long skirt.

Dakkar hurried as she dashed round a rocky outcrop. He leapt over a boulder and glanced around. She'd vanished!

A footstep behind him warned Dakkar, but he was too slow. He spun round to see her holding up a smooth rock with both hands.

'I told you to leave me alone!' she yelled, bringing the stone down on his head.

Pain lanced through Dakkar's skull as he staggered back, tripping over. Overbalancing, he landed painfully and lay dazed and blinking. He glanced up to see the blurred image of Mary Anning's boots disappearing across the pebbles.

Dakkar lay still, his head thumping. He groaned, putting a hand to his scalp. A goose egg of a lump grew there. Dakkar groaned again and clambered to his feet. Stumbling over the rocks, he headed after the now distant figure. His head whirled and the horizon seemed to see-saw in front of him.

Mary hurried along the shore, still some distance from Dakkar. His head began to clear although the lump pulsed with pain. The shore grew narrow here and the cliffs grew sheer. Dakkar could tell this wasn't a place that many visited. The tide would rush in here, cutting anyone off from the town. He blinked and shook his head. She'd vanished again.

He stopped and scanned the cliff. A crack just about large enough for a man to squeeze through scarred the cliff face.

'I wonder . . .' Dakkar muttered to himself.

He hurried to the gap and peered into the darkness. Something moved in the shadows and a mechanical hissing and clanking filled the air. Taking a breath, Dakkar squeezed in through the fissure.

The cave opened up inside, allowing him room to stand. Dakkar's eyes became more accustomed to the dim light. Mary Anning stood in a strange metal cage, her mouth open and eyes wide. She clanged the door of the cage shut but Dakkar leapt forward and wrenched it open.

'Don't!' she screamed, pulling back at the door. 'It's dangerous! Any minute now it'll –'

'It'll what?' Dakkar snarled. 'Tell me what's going on!'

'Just get away!' she snapped, and she slammed the door closed again.

Dakkar dragged it open and jumped in before Mary could stop him.

'What on earth –' Dakkar began, but the hissing grew louder and more urgent, steam filled the room and Dakkar felt his stomach lurch.

The cage gave a jolt and then, with a rending of metal, the door bent inwards, crumpling as the cage began to fall.

'What have you done, you buffoon?' Mary shrieked above the squealing metal.

'We're falling!' Dakkar yelled.

He gripped the bars of the cage as it plummeted. The walls of a shaft rushed past. He could smell sulphur and the roar of the steam filled his ears. Mary stood pressed into a corner of the cage, fear etched on her face.

'It don't normally go this fast,' she shouted above the rush of steam and air. 'You've broken it!'

'What's happening?' Dakkar bellowed.

'Like you said,' she yelled back, 'we're goin' down! But you've messed it up, 'aven't you?'

The cage continued its descent. Dakkar and Mary clung to its sides, helpless. Sparks leapt from the crumpled door as it scraped down the rocky wall of the shaft. They both flinched as the whole frame clanged and bucked against the side. *Think*, Dakkar told himself. *Breathe slowly and think!*

'Is there any kind of lever?' Dakkar yelled over the roar in his ears. 'A brake maybe?'

'I dunno!' Mary scowled back.

Dakkar examined the cage. It was a rectangular box of solid metal bars with a roof and floor. It fitted almost flush with the shaft down which it was hurtling. Wheels at the side of the cage should have kept it level and stopped it snagging the sides but the door had knocked it out of line and now it rattled and clattered against the stone.

'It's designed to travel up and down this shaft.' Dakkar edged round to Mary. 'It must have controls of some kind!'

He pushed her aside to reveal a red lever sticking out of the frame of the box.

'You were hiding that,' Dakkar said above the screech of metal.

'Don't pull it,' Mary shouted. 'Who knows what'll happen at this speed!'

'Nonsense.' Dakkar spat and jagged the lever down.

Dakkar felt weightless as the ceiling of the cage came down to meet him. His head smacked against the hard metal and then he fell back down to the floor. Mary flopped on top of him. They had come to a dead stop.

For a moment they lay listening to the echoes of their gasping breath vanish up to the surface.

'There,' said Dakkar, grabbing the lever and pulling himself up. 'See? Nothing to worry about.'

A gentle, metallic *ping* seemed to mock his statement. Dakkar watched in slack-jawed horror as the pin holding the handle in place slid to the floor and vanished over the edge. Then the lever came off in his hand.

'That's not good,' Mary whispered, staring at him.

The whole cage creaked and shuddered. With a bang that threw Dakkar back to the floor, the cage continued its downward journey, faster this time. The handle spun from Dakkar's grip and bounced off the wall, whirling back and nearly clipping his temple as he reached to grab it.

The cage thumped the shaft at regular intervals now, slowly twisting out of shape and becoming more unstable. Dakkar stumbled across the metal box, knocking Mary to the floor as he tried to steady himself. He pushed the handle back into its place, jamming it down.

Sparks fountained from the brake behind the lever and the handle shook, numbing Dakkar's arm. Slowly, the handle slid off the bar that held it. Dakkar desperately tried to push it back on, ignoring the friction heat that glowed from the metal. More sparks flew from the brakes, lighting up the shaft.

Mary threw herself towards Dakkar, and for a second he thought he was going to have to defend himself. Her hands pushed on the brake too, however, and gradually the cage began to slow even more.

Dakkar's heart pounded. Steam boiled up around them. The whole shaft seemed to rattle. It had grown hot and stuffy.

The roof of the cage gave a deafening clang as it snagged on something that ripped it out.

Dakkar's arms ached and his hands burned with holding the increasingly hot metal lever. Mary gasped next to him.

'We must be near the bottom by now,' she panted, sweat rolling down her brow.

Light glowed around the edge of the floor and the cage exploded in a scream of tortured metal. Dakkar's feet hit hard ground. Pain speared up his legs, through his knees and up into his jaw. He tasted blood in his mouth and he stumbled forward, out through a roughly hewn doorway. Mary leapt after him, leaving a tangle of metal struts and bars blocking the shaft.

'Well, there goes any hope of gettin' back up to the surface!' Mary said, slapping her hands at her sides.

But Dakkar didn't reply. He stood, open-mouthed, staring at the scene before him.

He was gazing into dense, green jungle.

CHAPTER ELEVEN
THE UNDERWORLD

'It's a . . .' Dakkar pointed at the tall ferns and trees that filled his vision. Above him, clouds swirled and crackled with lightning. Insects buzzed through the air and creatures chirped and croaked from the undergrowth.

'It's a forest,' Mary said, putting her hands on her hips. 'And thanks to you we're stuck here!'

'Thanks to me?' Dakkar said, raising his eyebrows.

'If you hadn't followed me and pulled the door open, I'd have been fine,' Mary said, her cheeks blazing red. 'But, no! You had to go and wreck the cage. Now we can't get back up!'

She walked over to a rotten tree stump and pulled out a water bottle with a long strap, a knife, a satchel and then a short stubby rifle with a wide barrel. Dakkar stared once again.

'What's the blunderbuss for?' he said, blinking.

'In case we meet the owner of your precious claw!' she

replied, looking over his head and into the dense jungle. 'Or one of his friends.'

A distant roar punctuated Mary's sentence and made Dakkar swallow hard.

'What is this place?' Dakkar demanded.

'We're deep underground,' Mary said. 'I dunno how this forest got here but here it is. I found it by accident some time ago.'

'But you didn't build the ingenious descending cage?' Dakkar said, frowning.

'No.' Mary sounded defensive, as if she could have if she'd wanted to. 'I dunno who made that but I ain't never seen anyone else down 'ere. Anyway, that's all a bit after the fact now that you've destroyed the bloomin' thing!'

They both turned to look at the entrance to the shaft. It was carved in a rock face that rose straight and sheer to the clouds. Dakkar thought he could see tiny black shapes flying high above them.

'It wasn't my fault,' Dakkar muttered to himself. 'Why did you run away from me?'

'Well, you jumped on me, to begin with,' Mary said, her cheeks reddening. 'And when you showed me the claw, I thought maybe you knew about down here and I was in trouble or somethin'.'

Dakkar tried to make sense of Mary's story. 'But if –' he began.

'Look, are we goin' to stand 'ere all day gossipin'?' Mary cut in. 'Only, I want to make sure everythin's all right down 'ere and maybe we can find another one of them cages somewhere.'

She started to walk towards the edge of the forest. Dakkar hesitated for a moment, watching Mary disappear into the thick foliage.

'You goin' to stay there, then?' Mary called. Dakkar could still hear twigs snapping under her feet and see the leaves waving. He hurried after her, pushing branches and ferns aside.

'What are you checking?' he called after her when he saw the back of her bonnet again.

'Keep your voice down,' she hissed, turning and scowling at him. 'Look.'

They had entered a small clearing. The giant ferns and trees reared up all around them, making the light from above green. A cairn of stones stood at the centre of the clearing. Mary stalked over to it and looked all around, giving a sniff.

'All fine,' she muttered.

Dakkar picked up one of the stones. A spiral pattern curled around it.

'It's like a snail shell,' he said. 'Only it's stone.'

'There are some prize specimens,' Mary said, grinning. 'Not bashed up by the sea. I take a couple up every now an' then to sell 'em to the lords and ladies who visit. They pay a fortune.'

'You come down here for *these*?' Dakkar snorted, throwing the stone back on the pile.

'Careful!' Mary said. 'Money mightn't be a problem to

the likes of you, Mr Prince of Dakkarkan or wherever you said you come from, but those rocks put food on my old mam's table.'

'I'm sorry,' Dakkar said, feeling his cheeks flush. Sometimes he forgot how privileged his life was, even living with Oginski; the count never wanted for money.

Mary just stared at him and raised her shotgun. Dakkar's stomach lurched and he raised his hands.

'Look, I said I'm sorry,' he said. 'I didn't mean to –'

'Get ready to duck,' Mary said in a low voice. 'Duck and run. NOW!'

Dakkar threw himself on the ground as Mary pulled the trigger. He saw her leave the ground as the explosion from the gun filled the clearing. An even more deafening roar answered the dying blast.

Turning, Dakkar saw an enormous yellow eye, rows of teeth the length of steak knives and a drooling red mouth. It was a huge lizard and reminded him of the beast he'd seen in Elba, but this one stood some ten feet high when it reared up. Dakkar scurried over to Mary. Pulling her up by the arm, he dragged her through the undergrowth. She stumbled after him, leaves and fronds whipping in her face. But Dakkar couldn't stop. The earth shook as the creature gave chase. Trees groaned and splintered as the monster thrashed through the jungle after them. Dakkar tripped over a root, pulling Mary down too.

'Get up, you idiot!' she screamed, dragging at his sleeve.

Dazed, Dakkar staggered to his feet and started running again. The giant lizard was gaining on them. Dakkar could hear its growling breath and smell the rank odour of rotten meat that surged ahead of it.

'We . . . can't outrun . . . it,' Dakkar panted, glancing desperately around for a place to hide, a hole in the ground, anything.

'That tree!' Mary yelled.

Ahead of them, the jungle fringed the thick trunk of an old fir tree. It soared above their heads but the branches stuck out at regular intervals, making it easy to climb.

The lizard roared again. Dakkar glimpsed red on its shoulder where Mary had winged it with the blunderbuss. It hadn't slowed down, though.

Dakkar reached the base of the tree and pushed Mary up as she leapt for the lowest branch. Leaves and saplings were torn aside as the lizard drew near. In a moment, it would reach Dakkar. He could see its claws now and the brilliant green of its scales between the foliage.

Mary cleared the first few branches and Dakkar hurled himself upward to the bottom boughs. The trees around them swished and the lizard's head grazed Dakkar's boot as he climbed up to the next branch.

'Keep climbing!' Mary screamed.

The lizard coiled itself for a leap. Dakkar could see its powerful back legs and wondered just how high it could jump. He dragged himself upward, glancing down in time to see the lizard spring up. Its snout and teeth grew larger as it hurtled towards Dakkar. The stink of the creature enveloped him and he leapt himself, ignoring the danger. For a moment, he felt weightless, expecting to be snatched back to earth by those vicious, snapping jaws. The next branch up drew near and Dakkar gripped it as tightly as he could, hoping that the weight of his body wouldn't break his grip. His shoulders burned as he swung on the branch, dangling like a tempting titbit for the lizard. But he was out of reach. The lizard snapped on thin air and then tumbled to the ground, falling heavily.

Dakkar's heart hammered against his ribs. He heard Mary give a nervous laugh and grinned up at her.

A low growl returned Dakkar's attention to the base of the tree. The lizard was back on its feet and glared up at them, growling.

'Now what do we do?' he said under his breath.

The monster wasn't going away. They were trapped.

CHAPTER TWELVE
TRAPPED

Mary Anning scowled down at Dakkar from her perch a few branches above him. Below, the huge lizard hissed and snapped. Every now and then, it would circle the thick trunk as if trying to find a way up.

'This is all your fault,' Mary said, throwing a pine cone at Dakkar. 'If you hadn't chased me down here, shouting like a lunatic, that lizard would never 'ave bothered.'

Dakkar snatched the pine cone from the air as it sailed past his head. 'You say the most obvious and pointless things,' he said. 'Of course the lizard wouldn't have chased us if we hadn't come down here.'

'You know what I mean,' Mary snapped, narrowing her eyes.

Dakkar looked down at the lizard. From his vantage point, he was able to take in more detail: the strong back legs that pushed the creature upright, the long tail that tapered to a point and seemed to act as a counterbalance to its huge head. Its tiny arms hung stubby and useless in front of it.

'What is that thing?' Dakkar whispered to himself.

'What do you think it is?' Mary said, launching another pine cone. This one missed entirely and bounced off the lizard's head, making it rear up and hiss. 'It's a big crocodile. I've seen pictures of 'em in a book.'

'I've seen real crocodiles,' Dakkar said, rolling his eyes. 'And they don't generally walk on two legs. Have you still got the blunderbuss?'

'Yes but I ain't usin' it up 'ere,' Mary said. 'It'd blow me out of the tree! I'm not savin' you from that monster by breakin' my neck.' She launched a pine cone at the lizard, clipping its nose and making it snap at the air with its razor teeth.

'Well, antagonising the beast won't help matters!' Dakkar grumbled.

'It makes me feel better, though,' Mary said, flinging another cone. The lizard caught the pine cone in its mouth, crunching it to splinters and shaking them out of its mouth. 'Maybe it'll get fed up of being pelted with cones and go away.'

'Unlikely,' Dakkar replied. He heaved a sigh then looked up at Mary again. 'Do you have powder in that satchel of yours?'

'Course I do,' she said.

'Pass it all down here,' Dakkar replied. 'I've got an idea. Keep throwing things at it.'

Mary eyed him suspiciously but climbed down a few

branches and swung the satchel by the strap towards him. Dakkar grabbed it, hugging it to him in case it spilled its contents to the ground.

The creature clashed its razor teeth at them as Mary continued to drop pine cones on to its head.

Rummaging through the satchel, Dakkar found a case full of black powder for the blunderbuss, some lead shot, flints and some wadding. The powder case was flat and triangular with a spout at one end for pouring the contents into a gun barrel.

'Perfect,' he muttered, pushing the lead bullets into the powder case and shaking them so they mingled with the contents. He ripped the wadding into strips and poked them into the spout of the powder case.

'What're you doin'?' Mary called down, craning her neck.

'You'll see,' Dakkar replied, wedging the case full of powder between his knees so that the ragged strands of cotton poked up towards him. He took the flints and began scraping them together. Sweat slicked his palms and fingers, making Dakkar slip. He cursed as he scraped his skin. Blood trickled down on to the case as he struggled to get a spark.

'Why don't you use the flintlock on the gun?' Mary said, leaning forward and holding the blunderbuss out to him.

Dakkar pursed his lips but reached up, nearly dropping everything. He slung the satchel over his shoulder. Their movements made the giant lizard lash its tail and glower up at them.

Dakkar settled back on to his branch and pulled the lock back on the blunderbuss.

'Flintlocks work by striking stone against metal,' he said to Mary. 'The spark ignites the powder in the pan at the side of the gun which in turn causes an explosion in the barrel. That fires the bullet out. If I can just get the spark to light the wadding . . .' He held the side of the unloaded gun against the wadding and pulled the trigger. The gun clicked. He did it again and again, sweat dripping from his brow.

'I know how a flintlock works. Do you want me to try?' snorted Mary.

'Shut up,' Dakkar hissed, and pulled the trigger again. This time a small flicker quivered in the ragged cotton threads. He gave a grin and blew. Soon the heat of the burning cotton singed his cheek. 'Hey!' he shouted, half standing on his branch and waving the powder case. The lizard swung its head up and Dakkar thought it grinned at him.

Then the world turned upside down. Dakkar's foot slid on the bough beneath him. Mary screamed as he pitched down into open space. The lizard hissed and leapt up to meet him, its mouth a mantrap ready to spring. Once more the rancid stench of rotten meat overpowered Dakkar as the yellowed incisors grew ever larger. He hurled the flaming powder case as hard as he could into the gaping maw of the beast and then closed his eyes, expecting to follow it inside.

Pain stabbed across his chest and under his right

shoulder as Dakkar's fall was abruptly halted. He opened his eyes again.

The lizard stood beneath him, bobbing its head repeatedly as it choked on the powder case. Dakkar dangled from an overhanging branch by the strap of the satchel. He gripped it with both hands and swung his feet up, desperate to get back into the tree.

With a triumphant gulp, the lizard swallowed the powder case down and threw its head up towards Dakkar.

Dakkar scrabbled and kicked, managing to hook one knee over the limb from which he dangled. Now he hung upside down, his head perilously close to the scaly jaws of the creature.

A dull rumble brought the lizard to a dead stop. Dakkar fancied that its eyes widened. Then the tree shook and the clearing beneath it filled with fire and noise as the powder in the creature's stomach exploded. The blast swung Dakkar upward, coating him in a shower of guts and blood. Something wet and slimy slapped into his cheek. An eyeball bounced off one of the branches. Half a jawbone whirled mere inches past Dakkar's ear, like some gory boomerang.

The echo of the blast grew fainter. Bits of bone, hide and flesh thumped to the ground, followed by a shower of pine needles. A smell of charred meat hung in the air. Dakkar stared at the scattered remains that littered the clearing below. Somehow the blast had ripped through the upper part of the lizard, and the creature's lower abdomen and legs still stood, blackened and smoking. It would have looked vaguely comical if it hadn't been so disgusting. Mary peered down at Dakkar. Smoke from the explosion blackened her face and her eyes were wide.

'That'll teach 'im not to bolt 'is food,' she muttered, grinning.

Dakkar, still dangling upside down, broke into a giggle and couldn't help laughing along with Mary. Then the satchel strap snapped.

Dakkar tumbled, weightless, through the air. He scrabbled at the few low branches and twigs that whipped past him but gravity wrenched them from his feeble grasp. Then the hard ground punched the air from his lungs. He lay, gasping and dazed, staring up at the branches.

Mary's face appeared high up above him.

'Are you all right?' she called down.

Dakkar opened his mouth but no words came out.

A few minutes later, Mary appeared beside him.

'I think . . . we should try . . . and find another cage,' Dakkar said in a hoarse voice.

But Mary didn't reply; she only stared into the undergrowth. He pulled himself up into a sitting position, his bruised back stiff and aching.

The leaves and branches shook as something approached them – several somethings, judging by the movement all around them.

'Not more of the beasts?' Dakkar groaned, climbing to his feet and preparing to drag himself back up the tree again.

'Worse, I think,' Mary whispered, and pointed.

The green, glossy leaves of the jungle were swept aside by a dark, muscular arm. A human arm. Enormous and covered in fine, black hair. The rest of the giant pushed his way through the foliage and stood glaring at Dakkar and Mary. As tall as the lizard they had just slain, his thick black hair tumbled on to his shoulders and down to his waist. His dark eyes glittered under heavy brows. Animal skins covered his body, some scaly and reptilian, others the fur of some kind of mammal.

He raised the huge club in his hand and bellowed in an incoherent language. Suddenly more of the giants appeared, all clad in furs and skins, all carrying spears and clubs, all looking menacingly at Dakkar. The giants closed in on them.

'I don't think we'll be getting back to Lyme for some time yet,' Dakkar said.

CHAPTER THIRTEEN
GOG

The giant glanced around at the lumps of flesh scattered on the ground and the two legs standing at the base of the tree.

'Saranda!' He grunted, shaking his club at the smouldering ruin of the lizard. 'Ung!'

'What's he sayin'?' Mary said, her voice quavering. 'He sounds angry.'

'I don't know, do I?' Dakkar snapped back. He gave a bow to the giant and pointed at the lizard. 'Saranda!' he said, copying the giant.

The big man frowned and tilted his head to one side then stepped forward, jabbing a huge, stubby finger into Dakkar's chest. Dakkar gave a gasp and fell on to his backside.

'You,' he said. 'Kill Saranda?' He stabbed his finger at the lizard, a look of bewilderment on his face.

Dakkar stared up at the giant that loomed over him. 'Y-yes,' he stammered. 'I killed Saranda.'

The giant narrowed his eyes, jutting his big chin forward. Dakkar could see his crooked brown teeth poking over his cracked lips.

'Rarrgh!' the giant shouted. He said something else and the gigantic group pounced on Dakkar and Mary. A thick net made of vines dropped over them both. With the pull of a rope, it tightened round them, dragging them off their feet.

Rough hands grabbed and bundled them up, still in the net. Two poles slid through the net holes above them and they found themselves suspended, carried by four of the huge men.

'I think you said the wrong thing,' Mary whispered.

Dakkar kept quiet, watching the party of savage giants behind him picking up lumps of the charred lizard and stuffing them into sacks made of hide.

The jungle slid past as the party carried Dakkar and Mary along. Large, glossy green leaves, vines dotted with flowers and fruit, and scrubby, thorny bushes all scraped by as the giants moved with surprisingly little noise.

'Can you move your elbow just a little?' Dakkar whispered to Mary. 'It's digging right into my back.'

'No, I can't,' Mary hissed back, wriggling to illustrate how cramped she was.

'Where are they taking us?' Dakkar said, trying to arch his back to escape Mary's sharp elbow.

'To their camp, I reckon,' Mary said. 'I 'aven't a clue where we are now, though.'

The jungle grew thicker and Dakkar lost all track of

time. A deep growl in the depths of the forest made the party freeze. The biggest giant peered into the press of trees and muttered something, readying his club.

Silence fell over them. Dakkar held his breath, trying to see what the giant could see, but darkness and shadows swirled between the tree trunks.

Then Mary gave a scream as a huge head thrust out from the gloom, snapping its teeth, its yellow eyes shining. Dakkar's heart pounded. Trapped in the net, they were helpless. What if the giants just dropped them and ran? The chief giant skipped back, raising his club and then pounding it down. The night echoed with a sickening crack and the lizard crunched to the ground, dead.

They hurried on, not pausing to inspect the fallen monster. Dakkar looked back and saw that something squatted, already tearing at the carcass of the animal. *This is a deadly land*, he thought. *Everything is trying to eat everything else!*

As they journeyed on, Dakkar scanned the shadows of the jungle closely. He shivered, thinking that something could jump out at any second. They stopped several times on hearing growls or something thrashing about in the undergrowth nearby.

Finally, the trees and bushes thinned and Dakkar smelt woodsmoke. They entered a large clearing, dotted with huge huts made of mud and leaves. Fires burned between the huts and Dakkar could see more giants – women and children – tending to the fires. They looked like slighter and smaller versions of the men who had captured them.

Their brows were low and heavy, their noses large. Wiry hair sprang from their huge heads and hung about their fur-covered shoulders.

A crowd gathered around Mary and Dakkar. A confusion of curious faces, poking fingers and grunts made Dakkar flinch.

The men carrying the net dumped it on the ground, spilling Dakkar and Mary out. For a moment, Dakkar thought they would be trampled by the onlookers. He curled into a ball, covering his head.

The giants dragged Dakkar to his feet and, with Mary at his side, he found himself propelled across the clearing to a huge throne by a roaring fire. The chief giant sat on the massive chair, glaring at them.

'I Gog, Chief of Gulina People,' he said, raising his chin. He pointed at Dakkar. 'Who?'

Dakkar gave a short bow. 'My name is Prince Dakkar of Bundelkhand,' he said. 'This is Mary Anning of Lyme Regis. We mean you no harm.'

'I can speak for myself, you know,' Mary hissed.

'You stone girl,' Gog said, pointing at Mary. 'We watch . . . many days . . . you collect stones. Why?'

'I sell them,' Mary said. 'Up there.' She pointed to the clouds that swirled and crackled above their heads.

'Sell?' Gog looked confused. 'Sky?'

'Our people,' Dakkar said. 'They live up there.'

'*Praya vasadi agaza!*' Gog announced in a loud voice to the crowd that surrounded them. Laughter rippled across the clearing but Gog's smile dropped. 'You lie,' he said, banging his fist on the arm of the chair. His eyes darkened and Dakkar thought he saw pain in them. 'All small ones lie. *Lagu gara!*'

At the last words, three giants sprang up and grabbed Dakkar and Mary. Dakkar struggled but the iron grip on his arms did not break. The guards dragged them to a hut and threw them inside. Dakkar ran at the door but it slammed shut in his face, sending him sprawling back on the dirt floor.

'Well, this ain't so good,' Mary muttered, putting her hands on her hips.

Dakkar scanned the room. The hut was circular and very bare apart from a pile of animal skins that lay in a heap, forming a rough bed. He pressed his palms against the walls. They were solid and thick, offering no chance of escape.

'It looks like we're prisoners,' Dakkar said, examining the door. 'Unless I can cut through the reeds that bind the planks of this door.'

'That shouldn't be 'ard,' Mary said. ''Ave you got a knife?'

Dakkar rummaged in his pockets and found a small penknife. He paused. 'The only trouble is,' he said, pressing a hand on the door, 'what do we do if we get free?'

'Go home of course!' Mary said, her eyes wide.

'Do you know the way?' Dakkar said, arching his eyebrows at her. 'And would we survive that deadly jungle if we did find the right route back?'

'You're right, I suppose,' Mary said, pouting her bottom lip. 'What d'you suggest, then?'

'I'm not sure,' Dakkar said. 'Maybe we can persuade Gog that we aren't a threat. He might let us go.'

'"E didn't seem too fond of us "small ones", as he put it!' Mary said. 'Perhaps we could tell 'im that we've buried some treasure back where 'e found us.'

'I don't think he's that interested in treasure,' Dakkar said. 'Besides, think what he might do once he realised it was a lie.'

'Well, I'm not 'angin' around 'ere to be eaten – or worse – just cos you can't think of a plan,' Mary said, snatching the knife out of his hands. She began sawing at the dry reeds that bound the door together.

'Wait!' Dakkar said, leaping forward. 'Look!'

A pair of dark, gentle eyes peered through the gaps between the planks of the door. They were smaller and younger than Gog's or the other giants.'

'A youngster!' Mary said, poking a finger through the gap. 'Hello, littl'un. What's your name?'

'Careful,' Dakkar whispered. 'It may bite.'

'It's a boy, I reckon, and only a baby,' Mary said, laughing as the young giant hooked a finger round hers. ''E don't mean any 'arm.'

Mary pulled her finger back and the baby giant gave a snort and a giggle. Dakkar pressed his eye to another gap. The child sat outside the door, a small replica of its parents but still equal in height to Dakkar or Mary. His long, matted hair covered his shoulders and his fur wrappings hung a bit looser. He looked up at Dakkar and gave a gap-toothed grin. Dakkar couldn't help but smile back.

Dakkar scanned across the clearing. 'So many women and children,' he said. 'Where are all the men?'

'Huntin', perhaps?' Mary suggested, reaching out and tickling the baby's palm.

'How long have we been here?' Dakkar asked, glancing at the cloudy sky. 'Shouldn't it be dark by now?'

'We're underground,' Mary said simply. 'And it never goes dark.'

'But where does the light come from?' Dakkar said. 'How can there be a sky with clouds in it?'

'There's no sky,' Mary said. 'Look. It's just a solid bank of cloud. I reckon it's a gas of some kind.'

'A gas that glows?' Dakkar said, curious.

'I once saw a gentleman make an explosion usin' gas and a flame,' Mary said, her eyes wide. 'He was a natural philosopher. I took 'im some of my petrified shells and he showed me his workshop. Nearly blew it up, 'e did!'

'Explosions I can understand,' Dakkar muttered. 'They're common in mines where underground gas builds up, but to be constantly combusting like this? Amazing!'

'Do you think . . .' Mary began to say but something stopped her. The child had turned to look behind him and gripped her finger tightly. 'What's up, fella?'

Gunfire crackled from the forest and Mary cried out as the child scurried away, wrenching her finger.

Dakkar stared out as giants scurried this way and that. Screams filled the air. More gunshots rang out and Dakkar watched in horror as figures began to fall to the earth.

'They're killing everyone!' he gasped. 'Quickly – give me that knife.'

With trembling hands he sawed at the door's thick reeds, which seemed to be tough as iron. More gunfire echoed and then a deep hissing roar made Dakkar pause and stare out between the boards.

In the clearing stood a lizard, a biped, smaller than the one that had chased them up the tree. It pinned a wounded giant down with one powerful leg and sank its teeth into the poor man's neck. Dakkar stared in horror – the lizard was harnessed and bridled like a horse, and a man sat on its back, wearing the black uniform of Count Cryptos.

CHAPTER FOURTEEN
COLD FURY

Dakkar slashed at the door's bindings with trembling hands, pausing to rattle at the planks now and then in the vain hope that they had come apart.

'What're you playin' at?' Mary said. 'There's shootin' goin' on out there!'

'Those men are evil,' Dakkar spat. 'They're slaughtering Gog's people. We've got to stop them.'

'Stop them?' Mary said faintly.

'At last!' Dakkar hissed as the reeds finally snapped and the door sagged on one hinge. He gripped it and threw his weight backward, tearing the door out of its frame.

The scene outside horrified him. Giant bodies lay strewn around the camp. Fires smoked in the rush roofs of the huts. Dakkar swallowed hard and blinked back the stinging sensation in his eyes. Anger boiled up inside him.

Scanning around, he counted six mounted Cryptos guards harrying a circle of giants that strove to protect the remaining children. He noticed that the women had grabbed spears and clubs too. One Cryptos guard lay crushed under his lizard, obviously a victim of Gog's mighty club. Another lay further away, nearer the scrum, a huge spear pinning him to the ground.

'Dakkar, you can't!' Mary shouted behind him. 'It's too dangerous.'

'I'll not stand by and watch women and children being murdered,' he snapped, running over to the fallen guard.

Dakkar squatted down, snatching the rifle from the dead man's hands. He pulled the pistol from his belt and grabbed the powder horn. Then he backed into the hut, dragging Mary with him.

'Load this,' he said, pushing the pistol into her hands. 'If any guards come in here, shoot them.'

Once he'd loaded his rifle, he ran out into the clearing again. The Cryptos guards were occupied with attacking the giants and wouldn't expect an attack from behind. Even in the short time it had taken Dakkar to load the rifle, two more giants had fallen. He needed to use the element of surprise to fullest effect.

Glancing down, he saw that the other fallen guard's rifle lay primed and ready on the ground. The dead man held a round metal ball in his hand. *A grenade!*

Six guards, Dakkar thought, grabbing the grenade. *Two rifles and this. I'll have to shoot well!*

He straightened the fuse on the grenade and poked it into the fire that smouldered nearby. The fuse spat and flicked into life. Dakkar's heart pounded as he waited. If he threw it too soon, the men might have time to kick it away or rip out the fuse. If he waited too long, it would explode as he threw it, maiming or killing him. The spark ate through the black fuse. As it reached halfway, Dakkar threw the grenade as hard as he could.

The grenade whirled across the clearing and cracked one of the guards on the back of the head. Another turned as the bomb exploded with an ear-shattering bang. Shards of hot metal peppered the next guard, sending him flying from his saddle. The lizard he had been riding gave a shriek and fell on top of him, lashing its tail into a third rider.

Dakkar dropped to the ground and fired the first rifle. He grinned as his shot clipped the fourth rider, who fell. Dakkar snatched up the second gun.

The confusion had stunned the guards but also some of the giants, who cowered as the last roar of the grenade faded. But Gog had recovered and swung his huge club at the fifth Cryptos guard, sending him spinning from his mount. The guard landed on his back with a loud thud and didn't get up. Two female giants stabbed their spears into the lizard's throat, knocking it backward off its feet.

The final guard pulled out a pistol and pointed it straight into Gog's face. Everyone froze. The women held their spears level and Gog braced himself to die.

Dakkar gritted his teeth and squeezed the trigger.

The rifle jerked in his grip, numbing his shoulder and making him think he'd missed. A spurt of red in the man's arm told him he hadn't, and the pistol fell from his useless hand. Dakkar winced and looked away as the giants fell upon the wounded man, stabbing with spears and pounding with clubs.

Gog stood still and stared over at Dakkar. The giant's eyes burned with anger. Dakkar glanced around for the powder horn but saw only scattered ashes and the dead Cryptos guards. *He's going to kill me*, Dakkar thought as the giant turned and stamped towards him.

Dakkar stood, gripping his empty rifle in trembling hands. *Maybe I can use it as a club*, he thought hopelessly.

Gog towered over him now, staring down and frowning. Dakkar stiffened and met Gog's gaze. *At least I'll die with dignity*, he thought, *as a prince should!*

Then, to his surprise, Gog squatted down and brought his face close to Dakkar's.

'You hate Rohaga too,' he said, pointing at the fallen rider. It was a statement, not a question. 'You save Gog's life.' He bowed his head and thumped a fist to his chest. '*Bukkah!*'

Dakkar bowed back. 'My pleasure,' he said. He tried not to think of the riders. Although he'd only wounded them, some had already died at the hands of the giants and the other riders would too. There was nothing he could do about that.

'W-el-come.' Gog rolled the word around in his mouth. Then he glanced at the bodies scattered about them.

Dakkar felt a pang of sadness at the carnage. About

twenty giants remained. Dakkar counted six men, eight
or so children and six women. Dakkar could hardly bear
to look but estimated that around thirty giants had fallen.
The survivors of the attack hurried from body to body,
hoping to find life. Women wept and sometimes a giant
would cry out in rage, beating the ground with his fists.
Some huts blazed and cooking fires lay scattered across
the clearing.

'Cryptos hunts your people?' Dakkar said. 'The
Rohaga – they try to kill you?'

Gog paused for a moment, then nodded. 'Always. They
kill the Sarba tribe. They kill all. We . . .' Gog searched
for the word. 'We hide.' He wandered off, pausing at the
body of a friend.

Mary stood at the door of the prison hut, her face pale
and drawn. The pistol hung in her fist. Dakkar walked
over to her and prised the gun from her grip.

'It's terrible,' she whispered.

'This is what Cryptos does,' Dakkar said, almost to
himself. He'd seen the ruthlessness of Oginski's brother
and his own father, the Rajah of Bundelkhand, taking
life, but this went beyond anything Dakkar had ever
experienced. He thought of Oginski. *Was he this ruthless once?*

'We not stay,' Gog shouted over to him, whirling his
club over his head. 'Rohaga have found us. To caves!' He
pointed a blackened fingernail to a distant rocky outcrop
that poked above the treeline. '*Samblaya! A Khav Suum!*
More Rohaga be here soon. You come with us.'

Dakkar stood, uncertain for a moment, and glanced at Mary.

'Well, I'm not waitin' 'ere to be killed!' Mary snorted, hitching up her skirts and stamping over to Gog's side.

The remaining giants gathered food, pots, skins and weapons on to their backs. Dakkar hurried from one fallen rider to the next, salvaging rifles, pistols, powder and musket balls. The giants had smashed most of them but he managed to gather two pistols and two rifles and plenty of ammunition. In addition, he found a sharp knife and a machete for hacking down thick foliage. He passed a rifle to Mary, who slung it over her shoulder.

While Dakkar was searching for weapons, the giants lay the bodies of their dead in rows in the clearing. Dakkar rejoined the giants and watched Gog's people hurl the bodies of the Cryptos guards unceremoniously into the bushes.

Dakkar looked puzzled and Gog joined his thumbs together, flapping his fingers so that they looked like the wings of a bird. 'Gacheela take ours,' he said solemnly. He pointed to the pile of dead Cryptos guards. 'Rohaga. Saranda have them.'

'Sounds like being eaten by the lizards isn't good,' Mary said, pulling a face.

'Would you like to be?' Dakkar replied.

'If I was dead then it wouldn't matter,' she said, shrugging.

'I wonder what Gacheela is,' Dakkar murmured.

'A flying lizard is my guess,' Mary said, shivering. 'I saw

one once. A horrible thing with a long pointy beak full of teeth. Looked like the devil, all claws and batwings!'

Weeping, the party moved out of the clearing, their steps leaden. Dakkar and Mary followed in silence.

Time dragged on again and weariness weighed Dakkar's feet down. Mary looked exhausted too. She tripped over a root, bumping into Dakkar and waking him from a stumbling doze. In his waking dream, Oginski had been calling to him from his deathbed. Dakkar could see his mentor's pale face and pleading eyes. *Is he still alive?* Dakkar wondered. *How long have we been down here?*

Gog raised a hand and the party stopped so suddenly that Dakkar staggered into the legs of the giant in front of him. They had come to a cliff face with huge steps worn into the stone. High above them, Dakkar could see cave mouths dotting the rock.

Gog weaved in and out among his fellow giants and crouched down to talk to Dakkar. 'Cave is high,' Gog said. 'Climb on back. Gog will carry.'

Dakkar felt a flush of embarrassment but looked at the steps. Each one would require him to pull himself up using both arms and legs. It would be exhausting. Dakkar looked at Mary, who shrugged.

'Thank you, Gog,' Dakkar said.

Gog turned and Dakkar put his arms round the giant's thick neck. Gog's skin felt rough and bristly as the giant stood up, supporting Dakkar's legs.

Dakkar looked up at the caves as they climbed,

desperate not to show his fear. Gog moved swiftly, almost leaping from step to step, and Dakkar had to keep tightening his grip. Glancing back, Dakkar saw Mary clinging to the back of another giant. Behind her, the jungle spread out like a green sea. In the distance, Dakkar saw the canopy of trees shivering and moving where giant lizards made their deadly way. Then he glimpsed something else far off. It looked like a pillar of rock reaching up into the clouds.

'Here!' Gog announced, leaping into a cave mouth.

Dakkar found himself inside a large cavern with a sandy floor. A few ancient stalagmites poked up to the ceiling. Somewhere water trickled over pebbles but the cave looked dry.

Gog stooped again to allow Dakkar down. Dakkar stood, his head spinning for a second.

Mary wandered over to him as the rest of the tribe began spreading furs and stashing food in carved-out alcoves in the cave wall. One of the women clashed flints together over a ready-built fire, filling the cave with flashing sparks. Soon the smell of woodsmoke tickled their nostrils.

Dakkar looked up and blinked, transfixed by what he saw.

'What're you lookin' at?' Mary said.

'That,' Dakkar whispered, pointing up into the shadows of the ceiling. 'How did that get there?'

Dangling from the ceiling, by dried-out vines and creepers, hung a familiar shape. It looked huge in this enclosed space, like a small whale hung up on display after being caught. Brass rivets gleamed in the newly kindled firelight; polished boards reflected the dance of the flames.

'What is it?' Mary said, clutching Dakkar's shoulder.

'It's a submersible,' Dakkar said quietly. 'Designed by my mentor and his friend. She is called the *Liberty*.'

CHAPTER FIFTEEN
THE WHALE IN THE CAVE

'A boat that sails *under* the water?' Mary snorted. 'That's unbelievable.'

'Says the girl standing in an underground world full of monsters and giants,' Dakkar replied, folding his arms.

'Where did it come from, then?' Mary said, mimicking Dakkar's stance. 'And why is it hanging up in a cave all the way down here?'

'A friend of mine sailed her,' Dakkar muttered. His stomach churned. 'Georgia Fulton, an American girl, the niece of the inventor.' Dakkar ran over to Gog and pointed at the *Liberty*. 'Gog, where did you find this?'

Gog frowned. 'Girl came,' he replied. 'Said to keep safe.'

'A girl,' Dakkar said, his heart racing. 'With red hair?'

Gog nodded then a look of sadness crossed his face. 'She good, kind. She went to the Rohaga.'

'What do you mean?' Dakkar said.

Gog went to the cave mouth and motioned for Dakkar

to follow. The giant pointed across the top of the jungle to the distant column of rock.

'Rohaga live there,' Gog said, a hint of awe in his voice. 'Many of my people go there. Never come back. She go there. Never come back.'

'It must be a Cryptos fortress,' Dakkar murmured. He turned and looked up at Gog. 'When did she leave?'

Gog shrugged. 'Long time,' he said. 'Many Rohaga hunt us when she go.'

Mary appeared at Dakkar's side. 'You can't be thinkin' of goin' to that place?' she said, staring at him in disbelief.

'She's my friend,' Dakkar said, running his fingers through his black hair. 'I can't just leave her there. I've got to find her.'

'But we need to find a way to get back to Lyme,' Mary said, gripping his elbow.

'That's true, and I must get back to Oginski,' Dakkar said, his voice barely a whisper. 'But I can't walk away from Georgia. Anyway, she must have got here somehow – perhaps she knows another way out. You don't have to come – I wouldn't expect you to help.'

Mary scowled at Dakkar and put her hands on her hips. 'Then what are we waiting for?'

'It'll be dangerous,' Dakkar replied. 'Maybe we should wait here.'

'I know most of the creatures round these parts,' Mary said. 'I can guide you –'

'You guided me right up a tree last time,' Dakkar muttered, shaking his head.

'*You* wrecked our only way home!' Mary snapped, the colour rising in her cheeks. 'If you don't let me come, I'll just follow you.'

'But why would you want to come along?' Dakkar frowned.

'I bet whoever lives in that built the cage in the shaft,' Mary said with a shrug. 'Finding them is my best chance of getting out.'

'That's true,' Dakkar sighed. He could see that Mary wouldn't give up. He craned his neck and scanned the horizon. A thin ribbon of silver glistened among the trees. 'It's a river,' he said to himself, an idea forming. 'Gog,' he called to the giant and pointed at the *Liberty*. 'Can you bring that down for me?'

A flicker of indecision crossed Gog's face. Dakkar could read it with ease. Georgia had told him to keep it safe and now Dakkar was asking to look at it.

'You can trust me,' Dakkar pleaded. 'Georgia, the girl, she was my friend too. We've fought Cryptos – the Rohaga – before together.'

Gog paused for a moment more, then strode over to the stones that anchored the ropes holding the *Liberty* up above them. He called two other giants over and together they lowered the craft gently on to the ground. Dakkar marvelled at the giants' strength.

Soon, the *Liberty* sat, dusty and tilted to one side on her rounded hull. Dakkar clambered up and opened the front hatch. It smelt fusty. The light of the fire filtered through the portholes, casting long shadows as Dakkar slipped inside.

It all looked so familiar – a copy of his own *Makara*, the prototype small submersible. There was just a cabin below and the smaller captain's cabin above, which housed all the controls. Georgia's uncle, Robert Fulton, had built this craft at the same time as Oginski built the *Makara*, each helping the other as they came across problems or difficulties.

The floor sloped but Dakkar managed to clamber along. He swept his fingers through strands of cobwebs that stretched between the chairs and tables. He lifted the lids of the boxes at either side of the cabin. Empty. Normally these held Sea Arrows, projectiles with explosive tips that were fired by a powerful spring – with deadly effect. *Did Georgie have to use them?* Dakkar wondered.

He came to the back of the lower cabin and pressed his ear against the wooden wall that screened off the engine. Originally the *Liberty* had been powered by a cleverly geared clockwork motor. This had been replaced by a section of the Eye of Neptune, an electrically charged meteor fragment that Dakkar had rescued from the seabed near Cryptos's volcano lair. Dakkar could hear it humming quietly behind the wall. He smiled. The *Liberty* was in working order.

'It's like bein' inside a great big barrel!' Mary said, making Dakkar jump. He hadn't noticed her climb down behind him. He pursed his lips.

'The planks are fitted much more closely together,' he muttered, climbing up into the smaller cabin above.

He pulled a face as he beat the dust from the seat and

slid into it. He could see the curious faces of the giants peering in through the portholes, their faces blurred by the dusty glass.

Running his hands over the wheel, he thought of Georgia and Oginski. 'What if they're both dead?' he whispered.

'Who?' Mary asked, poking her head through the hatch below.

'None of your business!' Dakkar yelled, making Mary flinch. 'Who are you anyway? Why did you drag me down here?'

'I didn't drag you. You followed me, remember?' Mary snapped back. 'An' I'm the only friend you've got at the moment so just you bear that in mind!'

She disappeared back into the lower cabin and Dakkar heard her stamping back to the front hatch and climbing out.

Dakkar sat for some time gripping the wheel of the sub. An uneasy feeling sat in the pit of his stomach. As if he'd forgotten something or something wasn't quite right. He shook his head and climbed through the upper hatch, which brought him out on to the very top of the Liberty.

Gog watched him from the fire, the flames reflecting in the giant's dark eyes. Dakkar wandered over and sat down next to him.

'You sad,' Gog said. He pulled a stick from the fire and rolled some lizard meat from it. 'Eat.'

Dakkar swallowed hard as he looked at the scorched flesh but he bit into it. To his surprise, it tasted good. He wasn't sure when he'd last eaten but he knew he was hungry.

'I want to find my friend,' Dakkar said, pausing before taking a second bite. 'I want to bring her back from the Rohaga.'

Gog paused, chewing thoughtfully. 'Many have died,' he said. 'Many friends taken by Rohaga.' He looked around at what was left of his tribe. 'Soon all Gog's people will be taken. This will end. Tomorrow we go to save Gog's tribe. You can come with Gog.'

'Who taught you my language, Gog?' Dakkar asked after eating the rest of the meat. 'Was it Georgia – the girl?'

Gog shook his head. 'Stefan,' he said, giving a deep sigh. 'He came here. Hungry. Dying. We fed him. Healed him.'

'Where is this Stefan now?' Dakkar said.

Gog pointed out of the cave and shook his head. 'He left,' he said. 'He tricked us. We built his big house. He bring more little men here.'

'The Rohaga?' Dakkar said.

'Yes.' Gog nodded. 'The riders. Now he hunts us.'

'This Stefan,' Dakkar said, watching Gog's haunted face in the firelight, 'did he have any other names?'

'Another name,' Gog agreed. 'Og . . . Og . . .' He struggled to pronounce the word.

'Oginski?' Dakkar said. 'Stefan Oginski?'

'Yes,' Gog said, poking the fire with a stick. 'That name.'

Dakkar sat back, his fears confirmed. *Another Oginski*

brother is here, Dakkar thought. *Another Count Cryptos is only a few miles away.*

'The river,' Dakkar said, drawing a squiggly line in the sand that covered the cave floor. 'It goes past Stefan's tower?'

'Yes. It deep . . . long,' Gog said, tracing a huge finger over the line in the sand. 'Full of danger.'

'But maybe with the *Liberty* we can use stealth and catch the Rohaga by surprise,' Dakkar said, his voice hollow. Gog frowned and Dakkar wasn't sure if he hadn't understood or if he didn't think much of the idea.

'Sleep,' Gog said. 'Then we go.'

'I don't think I can sleep.' Dakkar sighed but he felt the events of the day – or was it the night? – catching up with him. His eyelids were heavy, his limbs weak.

Gog dragged a musty fur to Dakkar and dropped it over him. Although he didn't really feel cold, Dakkar pulled it round his shoulders and over his head, blotting out the constant light from the cave mouth. In the distance something roared and hissed.

Georgia is down there somewhere, Dakkar thought. *Tomorrow I'll find her!*

CHAPTER SIXTEEN
GACHEELA

It was pitch black when Dakkar awoke. He felt pinned down. Somewhere close by, deep voices chanted – a single voice calling then several others grunting in response. Panic tightened his stomach as he lashed out with foot and fist. Light dazzled him as the heavy fur cover flew off and landed on the embers of the fire, sending grey ashes fluttering everywhere.

Remembering where he was, Dakkar snatched the fur before the remaining embers set it alight. The chanting continued and Dakkar realised that it was Gog and his men heaving the *Liberty* out of the cave and down the steep cliff face. Long, plaited vines held by three, grimacing, sweating giants stretched across the cavern and out of the cave mouth.

One of the giant children scampered over, offering him a strange-looking, spiky-leaved fruit. Dakkar smiled and took the fruit. The child gave a gap-toothed grin and hurried back to his mother, who sat in the shadows of the cave, sharpening a spearhead. Breaking open the fruit, Dakkar bit into the sweet flesh inside. It tasted good.

A cry from the men brought his attention back to the *Liberty*. Dakkar could picture her dangling halfway between the cave and the ground. One slip and she would crash to the earth, shattering in pieces. She was tough and could stand a battering from the sea, but a drop like that would crack her like an egg on granite.

Mary stood by the cave entrance, peering down. Dakkar joined her and craned his neck to see what progress the giants had made. The *Liberty* hung below them, swaying in the breeze. Gog stood on the steps, steadying her, and two more men on higher steps gripped the vines that held her, but they had all frozen.

Two enormous creatures glided past, only feet from Dakkar.

'Gacheela,' Mary whispered.

The flying lizards were every bit as horrible as she had said they were. Dakkar could see the leathery skin that formed wings between their scaly arms. Small, clawed feet poked out behind their plump bodies. Their long beaks lined with sharp teeth made them look like they were grinning. They reminded him of the dolphins he'd seen on his travels – but these creatures looked far from friendly. They circled, their wings fluttering on the warm thermals that drifted up from the jungle below. All the time they eyed Gog and the two men.

Dakkar hurried back into the cave and grabbed the

rifle he had scavenged from the fallen Cryptos guard. With trembling hands he poured powder into the barrel.

'Mary,' he shouted, 'come over here and help me load the other rifle!'

Mary hurried to his side and grabbed the gun.

The Gacheela had drawn closer by the time Dakkar and Mary returned. Gog stood, back pressed against the rock, as the huge lizard swept down towards him.

Dakkar pressed the stock of the rifle to his shoulder and took aim.

A sickening screech threw Dakkar off his aim and he glanced up. A third flyer had joined the other two. It looked bigger, and scars across its belly and neck told Dakkar that it was a veteran of many battles.

Dakkar had an idea. His timing had to be perfect but it might just work. He leaned against the edge of the cave mouth and trained his rifle on the new arrival. This Gacheela swooped above the other two, who had edged closer to Gog and the two tribesmen.

Holding his breath, Dakkar squeezed the trigger. The kick of the rifle numbed his shoulder and, for a moment, the smoke from the firing pan obscured his vision. But an angry squawk told him he had hit his mark. Now he saw the older bird spiralling down, a neat hole in its wing. It struck one of the smaller creatures, snapping and tearing at it as it fell. The second Gacheela sank its sharp teeth into its rival's neck and the pair of them tumbled below, bouncing off rocks and finally vanishing with a thump into the canopy of leaves.

Dakkar grinned at Gog and the others, but they stared up in horror. The remaining creature had seen Dakkar and now it hurtled towards him, screeching, claws bared.

'Mary, the rifle!' Dakkar yelled.

Mary threw the rifle and Dakkar reached to grab it but the beast thudded into him, knocking him to the ground. The world was reduced to a flurry of leathery wings beating at him and sharp claws tearing at his jacket. Dakkar kicked out, catching the creature in its gut and pushing it away for a second.

The giant men in the cave looked on helplessly, realising that if they let go of the ropes the *Liberty* would crash down below. Some of the women edged forward, jabbing with spears. The Gacheela snapped at them with its long beak.

Something flashed in the corner of Dakkar's eye. It was the machete he'd taken from the dead guard in the camp. Making a dash, he grabbed at the handle of the blade. The Gacheela bit at him, snagging his trouser leg in its teeth. Dakkar just had time to grasp the machete's blade when the lizard took three powerful hops back, dragging him out of the cave and into mid-air.

Dakkar's stomach churned and the world turned upside down. Suddenly the jungle was the sky and the clouds layered the earth. His hip and thigh burned as he dangled from the creature's mouth, suspended from a few threads of trouser leg. Dakkar's weight dragged the Gacheela down at first and its cries deafened him. Then it began to beat the air with its powerful wings and their descent slowed.

They swooped down. The tops of the trees whipped
Dakkar's face and shoulders. A branch clipped his elbow,
nearly knocking the machete from his grasp. He glimpsed
the forest floor far below through the leaves. Something
with a long neck and too many teeth snapped at him from
a passing branch. Dakkar felt its rancid breath on his
cheek and then it vanished as they flew on. A tearing
sound, followed by a slight jolt, told Dakkar that his trouser leg was ripping. The treetops began to rise away as the
Gacheela beat furiously. In a few seconds, they'd be
hundreds of feet up and Dakkar would fall.

If I fall now then maybe the trees will save me, he thought.
Any higher and I'm dead.

With a yell of rage, Dakkar pulled himself up, swinging
the blade as hard as he could. The Gacheela's squawking
collapsed into a liquid gargle as the machete bit into its
neck. Warm blood splattered down on Dakkar's face,
forcing him to screw his eyes shut. Suddenly he felt
weightless and the air rushed through his hair and ears.
Opening his eyes, Dakkar could see the beast's severed
head, still gripping on to the fabric of his trousers. The
body was spinning off in another direction.

Dakkar caught a brief glimpse of Gog's distant face,
pale and wide eyed, and then the trees engulfed him.

CHAPTER SEVENTEEN
THE RIVER

Branches slashed at Dakkar's hands and arms, then whacked into his back as he fell further into the jungle. He yelled out as thorns tore at his skin and clothes. A flock of tiny lizards nesting on a branch scattered in all directions, skittering over his chest and head as he crashed through them.

Then he stopped, bouncing like a puppet on a tangle of vines, being thrown gently back up into the air and eased back down again. He looked down at the floor of the jungle a few inches away and blew out a long breath.

Dakkar clambered down from the vines and groaned. His body ached and his skin stung from a criss-cross of cuts and scratches. Looking around, he found himself a few feet away from the base of the cliff. He shuddered. If the Gacheela had taken another direction, he might have been dashed against the rocks.

Gog's face appeared through the bushes. He gave a broad grin when he saw Dakkar and strode over to him.

'Dakkar . . .' Gog began, and tapped the side of his head.

'Mad?' Dakkar grinned back.

Gog laughed and gave Dakkar a playful push, sending him sprawling to the ground.

'I assure you, I didn't do any of that on purpose,' Dakkar said, struggling to his feet and rolling his eyes.

Mary appeared, accompanied by one of the women of the tribe. 'Are you all right?' Mary said, putting a hand to her mouth.

'I think so,' said Dakkar, stretching and wincing at the same time. 'No bones broken.'

'You were lucky,' said Mary, her eyes widening. 'I 'ad you down as a goner, for sure.'

'You still want to come along?' Dakkar said, raising his eyebrows.

Mary nodded.

'Then let's get moving,' he said, striding after Gog, who had set off back to the steps.

They accomplished the task of getting the *Liberty* down the cliff without further incident. Gog's tribe had woven a net of vines and poked long poles through the netting. It amazed Dakkar that, giants though they were, these huge men could carry the submersible between them.

The jungle closed in on them and Dakkar felt a sense of unease creeping up on him. The shadows seemed darker and he would flinch at every snuffle or grunt from the undergrowth. He gripped his loaded rifle tightly.

Behind him, Mary trudged along with her gun slung over her shoulder. She was quiet but seemed more at ease as they walked. *I suppose she's been down here often*, Dakkar thought. *She must be used to it.*

Sometimes the vegetation grew dense and Dakkar offered to hack through it with his machete. Gog nodded in solemn approval. Other parts of the route took in well-beaten paths – main thoroughfares for all manner of creatures, judging by the tracks.

After hours of marching and struggling through the jungle, they came to a clearing on the side of a wide river.

'It must be deep,' Dakkar said, looking across the smooth water. 'It hardly seems to be flowing.'

Weeds and lily pads covered the surface here. Huge dragonflies, some the size of Dakkar, buzzed lazily across the water.

Gog led the way to the riverbank and wrinkled his nose at the water. Dakkar craned his neck to see what Gog was looking for.

'Nakra!' Gog said, extending his arms straight and smacking them together in a childish impression of a crocodile. Dakkar got the message.

'There are crocodiles in here?' he said, copying Gog's sign. 'Lots?'

'One,' Gog said. He stretched his arms wide. 'Big. His river.'

'Great,' Dakkar muttered. 'Let's hope we don't meet Nakra.'

'Dari!' Gog said to the men carrying the *Liberty*, and pointed to the water.

The giants waded into the river still carrying the submersible. Soon she bobbed in the water, not far from the bank.

'We'd better test the *Liberty* before we go any distance in her,' Dakkar said. He leapt from the bank on to the deck and pulled open the hatch. The *Liberty* suddenly seemed alive, rolling a little as as if to welcome him aboard as he climbed inside. It still smelt stale and dusty in the lower cabin. He climbed into the upper cabin and sat in the captain's seat. He turned a dial in the centre of the steering wheel and the Voltalith began to whine. A dull thud shook the boat and Dakkar heaved a sigh as Mary's voice rang up from the lower cabin.

'Should I shut this hatch at the front?' she shouted.

'Yes,' Dakkar called back, and slid the drive lever to *Full Ahead*. The engine hummed more loudly and he smiled as the *Liberty* began to push through the thick weeds that clogged the surface.

Mary appeared behind him. 'Are you goin' underwater?' she said, a slight smile on her lips.

'I might,' Dakkar said, turning to look out of the front portholes.

The river stretched ahead of them, wide but overhung with trees and creepers. Here and there, a fish would suddenly leap, breaking the surface and snatching an insect from the air.

'I've never been this far out,' Mary said, pressing her nose against the glass. 'I always stayed near the shaft.'

'I don't blame you,' Dakkar muttered.

They were out in the centre of the river now. Looking to his left, Dakkar could see Gog and a couple of his men staring at them. He grinned and turned the ballast wheel. Immediately water gushed into the cavity in the hull of the craft and she began to sink. Mary gave a shriek as bubbles gushed around the portholes and they were plunged into a shadowy, green world.

'We're sinkin'!' she screamed, gripping Dakkar's shoulder.

'I know,' Dakkar said, smirking. 'I thought you wanted us to.'

'It's beautiful!' Mary gasped as she stared out at the silver fish that flashed past the *Liberty*.

Something snake-like squirmed through the mud on the bottom, sending up a brown cloud of sediment. Small crayfish landed on the deck in front of the porthole, threatening with their pincers before the current dragged them away.

Dakkar steered the *Liberty* round in a circle and then blew the water out of the ballasts. Soon they bobbed on the surface. Dakkar climbed out of the top hatch and sat on the upper deck. He raised his hand and waved to Gog, who waved back. Mary climbed up and popped her head out of the hatch.

'It's so quiet,' Dakkar murmured. 'If we were at sea now I'd feel relaxed, but here it seems like we're waiting for the next thing to spring up and try to eat us.'

'Can we get back to the bank now?' Mary asked, glancing around.

'You're right,' Dakkar replied, climbing inside the *Liberty*.

When they were both back inside he pushed the lever to *Full Ahead* and eased the craft into shore. The *Liberty* nosed the bank gently, rocking slightly as she did. Dakkar threw her ropes to Gog, who tied them round a tree trunk.

'We rest,' Gog said, pointing at the fire that his men had lit.

Dakkar grinned at the sight of freshly speared fish hanging on sticks over the flames.

'Better than lizard,' he muttered to Mary, who grinned back.

They ate and slept around the fire, two men keeping guard. Dakkar stared out at the *Liberty* sitting on the water and wondered about Georgia. *What brought her down here?* Dakkar shook his head. He knew how impulsive she was – and what a fighter too. Judging by the dust and cobwebs in the *Liberty*, some months had passed since she had left for the tower.

Dakkar began to doze but a deep splash snapped him to wakefulness. One of Gog's guards had noticed the sound too and crouched near the water's edge, spear at the ready. Dakkar rubbed his eyes and climbed to his feet. He crept to the riverbank.

Something splashed again. Dakkar thought he had glimpsed a tree trunk or a branch drifting downstream, but the surface of the water lay clear apart from the weeds and broad lily leaves. He shook his head. Gog's guard shrugged his huge shoulders and went back to sitting on some giant tree roots that snaked into the water.

Dakkar went back to the fireside but sleep evaded him. He couldn't escape the feeling that someone – or something – was watching them.

CHAPTER EIGHTEEN
NAKRA

Fronds of river weed swayed in front of Dakkar as he steered the *Liberty* downstream. Here, the water was green with algae and vegetation. He feared the propellers would become entangled in the thick strands of plant matter that grew like a forest from the river bed.

'Why are we goin' so slowly?' Mary grumbled at his side. She had insisted on travelling with him rather than following with Gog and his tribesmen on the riverbank. It made sense but that didn't stop Dakkar from wishing her on the bank with the others.

'I have to be careful here,' Dakkar said through gritted teeth. 'I can barely see where I'm going. Do you want me to run her aground or hit a rock?'

'What's this do?' she said, ignoring his reply and turning the crank handle above his head.

'Leave it!' Dakkar snapped, pulling her hand away. 'If you must know, it's called a friction wheel and it creates an electric charge. If you turn it twenty times and then press that red button, it sends an electric current through the water around the *Liberty*.'

'Oh,' Mary said blankly. 'What's a lectrick?'

'Electric,' Dakkar said, emphasising the E at the beginning of the word. 'It's . . . it's like lightning.'

'I was struck by lightnin' when I was a baby,' Mary said, giving a grin. 'The two ladies with me died. I nearly did too but they say I came back to life. That's why I'm so special, so my old mam says.' Her voice trailed off.

They both stared out of the window. Dakkar pictured Oginski lying in his bed. *He's getting better*, he tried to tell himself. *He's not dead.*

'We'll get back to Lyme all right,' Dakkar said, and gave Mary a brief, brittle grin.

She opened her mouth to say something but the *Liberty* lurched to one side, sending her tumbling into Dakkar and knocking him out of his seat. The two of them fell against the walls of the craft as she rolled on to her side. Dakkar threw himself back into the seat as the *Liberty* righted herself.

'What was that?' Mary said, staggering to her feet.

'I don't know,' Dakkar replied, peering into the green soup that swirled before his porthole, 'but there's something out there.'

A dim shape receded into the distance ahead of them. Even in the green mist, Dakkar could tell it was huge.

'It must have swept past us,' Mary said, her voice barely a whisper. 'D'you think it was that Nakra thing that Gog talked about?'

'Very possibly,' Dakkar muttered, watching the huge shadow vanish.

He brought the *Liberty* to the surface, where Gog and his tribesmen stood on the bank. Dakkar popped his head out of the top hatch. 'Did you see anything?' he called to the shore.

Gog just pointed, his eyes wide. Dakkar followed his gaze and gave a muffled oath.

The water further downstream boiled as something enormous slithered around in the river. He watched as what looked like a cross between a tree and a whale powered back towards the *Liberty*. Even from this distance, Dakkar could see it was a colossal crocodile.

He slid back down into the *Liberty*, slamming the hatch behind him. 'Why does everything here have to have so many teeth?' he spat as he slammed the craft to *Full Ahead* and steered her towards the riverbank.

'What is it?' Mary said, pressing her nose to the port-hole. 'Oh my.'

'We should move into the bank,' Dakkar said. 'Hide in the weeds.'

But Mary had begun turning the crank handle. 'Twenty times, you said?' She grunted.

'I don't think that'll work,' Dakkar said, steering the *Liberty* through thick weed beds.

A shoal of silver fish rattled against the hull of the *Liberty* as they tried to escape the oncoming Nakra. Dakkar could see its gaping mouth and armoured body as it wriggled through the water. He'd seen crocodiles in his homeland but this had a large bulbous nose and its jaw seemed longer. It was also ten times as big as any crocodile he'd seen before.

'Well, hidin' isn't goin' to help,' Mary said, giving the wheel a last turn. 'It'll ram straight through our side.'

'Wait until the very last moment then,' Dakkar said, his voice hoarse.

The water hummed with the power of Nakra surging through it. It seemed to fill the whole river now and Dakkar braced himself for the impact.

Then Mary hit the red button and the green world outside turned electric blue. The *Liberty* rocked over as Nakra suddenly swerved aside and its belly scraped against the hull, shaking the whole craft. Nakra reared up out of the water then plunged back below, sending a blast of water against the side of the *Liberty* and washing her to the riverbank.

Dakkar gripped the seat, trying to stop himself from being thrown around the cabin as they rocked back and forth in the wake. He just glimpsed the crocodile swimming away, its tail lashing at the water.

'Did we kill it?' Mary gasped, jumping over to the porthole.

'I think we frightened it off for now,' Dakkar said, catching his breath. 'Let's hope it keeps its distance.'

The sound of splashing sent Mary reaching for the crank handle again but Dakkar grabbed her hand and pointed towards the porthole.

Outside, the giants had taken to the water and were grabbing at the fish that lay dead on the surface.

'I think you just provided dinner,' Dakkar said, a grin cracking his face.

Mary grinned back and soon their laughter rang out through the *Liberty* until it brought Gog's face to the porthole as he peered curiously at them.

Dakkar climbed out and smiled as Gog held up a fistful of fish.

'We eat well today,' Gog said.

They worked their way further down the river and paused to light a fire to cook the fish. The fish tasted good but their cheer from earlier had evaporated.

'That crocodile swam this way,' Mary said as they sat in a clearing by the riverside. Trees leaned over the clearing, catching the woodsmoke in their boughs. 'It could try and get us again.'

'Nakra a coward,' Gog said, staring into the fire. 'He lies in water, waiting.'

'We need a few weapons,' Dakkar said, sharpening a length of branch that he'd cut from a nearby tree with his machete. 'I can use these instead of the Sea Arrows but they'll only be effective at close range.'

'Better than nothing,' Mary said, dragging a fingertip over the point of the stick.

'Little men have guns,' Gog murmured, tearing at a piece of cooked fish. 'We have sharp sticks.'

'We can use their guns against them,' Dakkar said, not quite believing his own words. 'If we can get into Cryptos's tower, we can take them by surprise.'

'There, many Rohaga,' Gog said. 'They watch.'

Dakkar thought for a moment, watching the flames flicker. 'Gog,' he said finally, 'you said back at the cave that the Rohaga had taken your people.'

'They work,' Gog grunted, pointing a finger in the direction of the tower. 'Stefan works them for long time. Digging, lifting, pulling and pushing. Until their life leaves them.' He gave a huge sigh.

'That's terrible,' Mary said, biting her lip.

'My own son,' Gog said sadly. 'His mother, taken.'

'I'm sorry, Gog,' Dakkar said, looking down at the ground.

'Do you know if they're all right?' Mary asked.

Gog shrugged. 'Gog want to save them but tribe depend on him,' he said.

Dakkar shook his head. At first glance, this giant seemed savage and stupid yet the more Dakkar got to know Gog, the more he admired him.

'But don't you see? We have friends inside the castle already,' Dakkar said, clapping his hands. 'Believe me, Gog. Your people will rise up if we cause enough confusion. I've seen it happen before.'

Dakkar thought back to the Qualar, a strange race of undersea people enslaved by the last Count Cryptos. It was they who had brought down Cryptos by fighting his guards.

'We will fight,' Gog said, lifting his head. 'Better to die than be slave.'

Dakkar was about to reply when a metallic click silenced him.

'Don't move,' said a voice from the riverbank.

They turned to see their giant guard frozen with fear, a rifle pointed straight under his chin. The Cryptos guard holding the rifle looked like a child next to the quaking giant. Behind him four more guards levelled guns at Gog, Dakkar, Mary and the rest of the tribe who squatted around the fire.

'Well, what do we have here?' the guard grinned, pulling back the hammer on his rifle.

CHAPTER NINETEEN
THE TEETH OF A DILEMMA

Dakkar froze, his hands slightly raised. He glanced around, hoping to see one of Gog's men concealed in the bushes, but they all sat around the fire, eyes wide and focused on the rifles.

Two more guards sidled from concealment at the river's edge. *That's seven*, Dakkar thought. *There's eight of us but our rifles aren't loaded. We don't stand a chance.*

'What's your business with these savages?' the head guard snapped at Dakkar. 'What are you doing here?'

'They're my friends,' Dakkar sneered, folding his arms. 'I'm on a sightseeing tour!'

'Keep a civil tongue in your head, boy,' the guard said, jostling the gun. 'I've a mind to shoot you dead and take your carcass to my master. He'd be very interested.'

'Fool,' Dakkar growled back, lifting his chin. 'Once your master knew who I was, he'd have your head for killing me!'

The guard frowned but lowered his rifle slightly. 'So who are you?'

Dakkar didn't reply. Instead he stared at the shadow that grew under the surface of the river behind the Cryptos guards.

'You haven't answered me,' said the guard, taking a step forward.

Two huge nostrils, followed by two yellow eyes, appeared above the water as Nakra slid towards the river-bank. Dakkar glanced at Gog, who gaped at the growing mass behind the Cryptos guards.

'I think he's wastin' your time,' said one of the other men.

Dakkar's mind whirled. *Should I warn them?* he thought. *When Nakra comes on land, we'll all be in trouble.*

The reptile's head broke the water and its snout touched the sandy side of the river.

'I won't ask you again,' the Cryptos guard said through gritted teeth.

'Behind you,' Dakkar said, pointing.

'What?' the guard snapped.

'Nakra,' Dakkar said, his eyes widening. 'Behind you.'

The crocodile filled the bank behind them now, like a wall of teeth and muscle. One of the rearmost guards turned and screamed, firing his rifle into the hide of Nakra. The reptile angled its head and clamped its teeth around the man's ribcage. Dakkar glimpsed the spurt of red blood and heard the crunch of bone before he averted his gaze. The other Cryptos guards realised the danger

they were in now and fired at the crocodile's head. It
hissed and flinched back as each shot found its mark.
Then it powered forward, sending river water spraying
across the clearing. Its tail lashed across the open space,
knocking the guards off their feet, sweeping the fire and
the fish into the bushes. Dakkar hurled himself at Mary,
pushing her out of the clearing and into the undergrowth.
Some of Gog's men managed to leap over the huge tail
but others fell, getting clipped as it swung back again.

Two of the Cryptos guards lay groaning, their legs
broken. The other four fumbled for powder and bullets,
shuffling away from the approaching Nakra. It slammed
its clawed foot down on one of the stricken men, making
him scream out loud. The other had managed to load his
rifle again and fired into the crocodile's underbelly.

Nakra gave another hiss and turned, snapping at him.
The crunch of the crocodile's closing jaws cut the man's
scream short.

The remaining four Cryptos guards had reloaded but
looked from Gog and his tribesmen to Nakra, uncertain
on whom to fire.

Gog hurled his spear over the heads of the men, sending it straight into the open mouth of the reptile.
Reassured that Nakra was the main threat at the moment,
the Cryptos guards unleashed another volley at the crocodile. The bullets thudded into the reptile's thick skin.

Gog's tribesmen hurled their spears; some hit their
target but others clattered off the tough hide. Gog's
men grabbed stones and some smouldering branches

that had been scattered from the fire. They flung them at Nakra, bombarding it while the Cryptos guards reloaded their rifles.

Once more the bullets found their target and Nakra had had enough as, slowly, the huge crocodile began to drag its bleeding body back to the river.

'Reload, men!' the leader of the Cryptos Guard shouted. 'Get these savages before they get us!'

But Gog had anticipated what would happen. He grabbed the leader by an arm and a leg and threw him across the clearing. With a yell of terror, the man hurtled towards the retreating Nakra. The creature leapt up, grabbing the screaming man by the leg, then slid into the water. The surface of the river bubbled and frothed red for a moment and then all went quiet.

The remaining three guards looked at each other then dropped their guns and ran into the bushes, pursued by Gog's men.

'They go back and warn others,' Gog said solemnly. 'They must die.'

Dakkar shook his head. 'We could take them prisoner,' he said.

'And leave them tied up out here?' Mary said, her hands on her hips. 'That would be worse than murder.'

'We could take them with us, question them,' Dakkar said, trying to blot out the sounds from the jungle as the giants caught up with the guards.

'They would kill *us*,' Gog said simply, and walked down to the riverbank.

Dakkar followed. The *Liberty* bobbed to the side of the bank, moored to the thick trunk of a tree that leaned out over the river. Blood stained the water and tiny fish darted through the red clouds, finding nourishment where they could. Dakkar shivered.

'Will Nakra leave us alone now?' he wondered aloud.

Gog nodded.

'I don't like this land, Gog,' Dakkar said. 'Every day is a fight for survival. So much killing and death.'

Gog shrugged. 'Nakra only hunt food. Land fine until little men came along. They kill for no reason.'

'When we get rid of Cryptos, then it will be fine again,' Dakkar said, trying to reassure Gog.

'No.' Gog shook his shaggy head. 'Men know now. They come again and again.'

A grim silence hung over the rest of the journey. Gog and his warriors picked their way through the undergrowth while Dakkar and Mary sat in the *Liberty*, drifting along the surface with the current.

The thick vegetation along the riverbanks denied Dakkar any chance to take in his surroundings other than the vines and tree trunks, creepers and broad, leathery leaves. Life teemed all around them. Lazy, droning flies buzzed through the green canopy above them and tiny lizards leapt from branch to branch. Distant roars echoed across the treetops but sounded far enough away not to pose an immediate threat.

Soon another sound mingled with the strange hoots

and cries of the jungle creatures. A distant booming and swishing of waves.

'The sea?' Mary said, frowning.

'I hadn't really thought about it,' Dakkar said, half laughing. 'Of course rivers run into seas but how can there be a sea down here?'

As they rounded a bend, the river widened before them. Dakkar's mouth hung open at what he saw.

The land flattened out and vegetation abruptly thinned as the river opened into a shallow estuary cutting through a flat plain. Steaming pools of water dotted the expanse, and beyond it a rolling black sea. At the very mouth of the river a wooden stockade surrounded a soaring tower.

It took Dakkar's breath away. The walls were made of huge stone blocks and massive beams of wood. Round windows dotted the sides as the square tower reached up and up until the dark, grumbling clouds above them shrouded its top.

'I've never seen such a tall building,' Dakkar gasped. 'Even St Paul's cathedral in London isn't that big.'

'It's amazing,' Mary whispered, gazing up.

'We'd better get out of sight before we're spotted,' Dakkar said, steering the Liberty towards the bank.

The reeds scraped along the hull of the sub as Dakkar landed her in the last clump of dense foliage that clung to the river's side. Mary and Dakkar climbed out to find Gog and his tribesmen crouched among the bushes, their eyes wide with fear. They had never been so close to the tower since Stefan had started hunting them down. Slowly, they picked their way through the forest to the edge of the clearing that surrounded the tower.

'How are we going to get in?' Mary asked the question that was written all over the giants' faces. 'The stockade wall around it is so high.'

'Many guards on wall too,' Gog agreed.

Dakkar nodded. Huge tree trunks, sharpened to a point at the top, stood side by side to form the stockade wall. Guards paced behind these, giving them a high vantage point.

'We need to get a closer look,' Dakkar said, running his fingers through his hair. 'Maybe we can find a blind spot or a weak area.'

Gog gave a nod. They set off towards the tower.

'It's quieter here,' Mary said in a hushed voice.

She was right. The eerie silence made every step sound alarmingly loud; every twig that snapped was a gunshot to their ears.

'Rohaga kill everything,' Gog snorted. 'Nothing go near tower.'

The forest had been partially cleared around the stockade, preventing them from creeping close. The canopy let more light in here where the trees had been thinned out.

'This whole area has been partly cleared,' Dakkar said, frowning. 'Why?'

'What do you mean?' Mary said, catching up with him.

'Wouldn't it be better to have thick forest?' Dakkar

replied, waving his hand at the hacked vegetation. 'That would be harder to get through, surely?'

'Or completely razed to the ground to stop people sneaking up,' Mary added, following his line of thought. 'Unless Cryptos wants people to try to sneak up . . .'

But Mary never finished her sentence. With a gasp, she vanished into the ground as if it had swallowed her whole. Dakkar spun round to see Gog disappear and then his tribesmen. Taking a step forward, Dakkar felt the soil under his feet shift and then his stomach lurched as the ground gave way beneath him.

He was falling into blackness. Then he hit something hard and knew no more.

CHAPTER TWENTY
TRAITOR!

'Wake up!'

Something struck Dakkar hard across the face.

'Wake up, or do I have to smack you again?' a voice snapped at him. A familiar American accent rang in his ears as sharp as the slap that still lingered on his cheek.

Dakkar blinked, half expecting to find himself sitting in the *Liberty*. His cheek stung and his head spun. Grey stone walls surrounded him and straw lay scattered on the floor. He peered up at the blurred figure in front of him.

'G-Georgia?' he stammered. 'Is that you?'

'Of course it is,' said the figure.

The darkness gradually receded and Dakkar recognised the angry, red-headed girl standing over him, hands on her hips.

'Thank goodness you're safe, I thought . . .' Dakkar began. Then he stopped. 'Georgia, what are you wearing?'

'What does it look like?' Georgia hissed, glancing down at her black Cryptos uniform.

It fitted her snugly, a stiff woollen jacket with matching trousers and shining knee-high boots. Dakkar could tell it had been made especially for her. She hadn't stolen it as a disguise.

He glanced around the grey cell. They were inside the tower, it seemed. Two guards stood at either side of a narrow door behind Georgia, rifles at the ready, their eyes steely.

'What's going on, Georgia?' Dakkar said, straining at the ropes that held him to the chair. 'Why are you wearing that uniform?'

'I'll ask the questions from now on,' she snapped, her emerald eyes flashing with anger. 'What do you mean by sneaking up on Count Cryptos's tower?'

'This is madness,' Dakkar hissed. 'What do you *think* I was doing? Paying a social call?'

Another blow from Georgia stung Dakkar's cheek. 'You're a fool for coming here,' she said, narrowing her eyes. 'The count will kill you, and serve you right!'

'And you'll let him?' Dakkar said, shaking his head. His face glowed with the heat of the blow and the anger that boiled up inside him. 'I came to rescue *you*!'

'I don't need rescuing, thank you very much,' Georgia snorted, her face reddening under her freckles. 'I'm doing fine by myself.'

'I can see that,' Dakkar said, his voice faint. 'But why? How did you get here?'

'Uncle Robert heard a rumour about strange sea monsters off the coast of Nova Scotia,' Georgia said. 'But he wouldn't go and investigate . . .'

'So you went alone,' Dakkar said, finishing her sentence. 'And followed them here?'

'I found myself here by accident after chasing Cryptos. They led me into an undersea tunnel that brought me here,' Georgia said. 'Stefan rescued me from certain death. He made me realise how corrupt the nations of the world up there really are.'

'And you joined Cryptos?' Dakkar said, incredulous.

'So what if I have?' Georgia snapped back. 'There's a war coming, Prince, and everyone will have to decide which side they're on.'

'A war?' Dakkar said, frowning. 'But what about your Uncle Robert?'

'A fool, like you,' Georgia spat. 'Has he searched for me? Does he even care? No. Too busy with his plans and projects. He's happy to make weapons but never uses them.'

'Then why hide the *Lib*–' Dakkar began to say, but Georgia slapped him again before he could finish.

'Count Cryptos will want to question you himself, I'm sure,' she said, staring deep into Dakkar's eyes. 'You're better off telling me all you know. He'll be harder on you.'

'Harder than you?' Dakkar said through gritted teeth.

'He's ruthless, Dakkar,' Georgia said, and Dakkar thought he saw genuine fear in her eyes. 'I managed to persuade him that you might have useful information or he'd have killed you when we took you from the pits.'

'The pits?' Dakkar said.

'Covered holes in the ground, deep and sheer-sided. They surround the tower,' Georgia explained. 'You fell into them. You were lucky – some have sharp spikes at the bottom.'

'What about the others?' Dakkar said, the blood draining from his face. 'Mary, Gog?'

'Safe, for now,' Georgia said. 'The giants have been set to work. Mary has piqued the interest of the count. He's intrigued by how she found her way down here unaided and how she made many return trips. He sees potential in her.'

'Potential?' Dakkar said, scowling.

'As an agent for Cryptos,' Georgia said, folding her arms. 'He knows that the Brothers Oginski are getting older. New blood is required.'

'Like you,' Dakkar muttered, his voice bitter. 'I was given that chance once, remember?'

'Yes, and you took it,' Georgia said, arching her eyebrows. 'For your own reasons.'

Is she trying to tell me something? Dakkar thought. He glanced at the two burly guards but they just glared back.

'But, Georgia,' he said in a low voice, 'you know I never actually joined them.' Dakkar had pretended to side with Cryptos in order to foil his plan.

'I don't think this Count Cryptos will make *you* the same offer,' Georgia said, her face stony. 'You've blotted your copybook, so to speak.'

'You were my accomplice,' Dakkar retorted.

'The count knows the truth – that I was duped by you,' Georgia said, shaking her head. 'Besides, he sees how committed I am to the cause now. He trusts me.'

'Gog's tribe,' Dakkar said, his eyes pleading with Georgia, 'they're almost all dead. Women and children too. Butchered by Cryptos. You can live with that?'

'And the English would treat them with more respect?' Georgia said, turning her back to Dakkar. 'My own country treats its native people in just such a way. Those who join us and work for us fare better.'

'The Qualar didn't do so well when they worked for the other Cryptos,' Dakkar said through gritted teeth. 'They were slaves.'

'I was hoping I could persuade you to join us and then persuade Cryptos that you weren't beyond hope,' Georgia sighed, heading for the door. 'I can see I'm wasting my time. Take him back to his cell.'

The two guards jumped to attention, then advanced on Dakkar. Untying the ropes, they dragged him to his feet, twisting his arms behind his back until he winced at the pain.

'Georgia, wait!' Dakkar called out, but Georgia had vanished.

'Keep quiet, boy!' one of the guards snarled.

The guards dragged Dakkar out into a corridor lit by the flickering of flaming torches that hung from brackets in the wall. Shadows danced on the rock, exaggerating the gaps between the huge stone blocks that made the tower. Cell doors lined the dank walls that Dakkar stumbled past, propelled by the two burly men. Behind, he could hear moaning and even cries of pain. Every now and then a distant rumbling shook the building. Dakkar glanced at the guards in alarm.

'You get used to that, boy.' The guard laughed. 'The count uses the hot-water springs for power. Some of them fire water high into the air. The screaming? That's just someone who didn't agree with the count.'

They came to the final door at the end of the passage and the guard loosened his grip to reach for his keys.

Dakkar wrenched his arm free while simultaneously swinging his head back at the guard behind him. Pain stabbed through his skull as his head caught the guard in the chin and sent him staggering.

Dakkar leapt high and landed a kick to the side of the second guard's head. The guard bounced off the wall and then collapsed in a heap, unconscious.

Spinning round to face the remaining man, Dakkar's heart fell at the sound of a metallic click and the sight of the barrel of the man's musket.

'Stand still,' roared the guard, 'or I'll blow your head off!'

The guard on the ground began to groan and slowly pulled himself to his feet.

'Proper little firebrand, this one,' the guard said, rubbing his head. 'Keep that musket trained on 'im.'

The man fumbled with the keys and pushed the door open. They bundled Dakkar into the tiny cell and hurled him to the floor. Dakkar sprawled, panting, as the door crashed shut behind him.

He lay still, taking in his surroundings. Chains hung from the stone-block walls and damp straw clung to the rough ground, smeared in the foul mud that coated it. Dakkar leapt up. Shadows shrouded the room apart from the shaft of light that shone in through the small barred window above his head, but he could tell that he was not alone.

'You fight well,' a voice said in French. 'Keep that spirit, mon ami. You will need it.'

Dakkar squinted through the darkness. A dim shadow sat in the corner of the cell. A man, stocky framed and dressed in a dirty, ragged uniform of blue.

'Who are you?' Dakkar said. The voice seemed vaguely familiar but he couldn't place it. 'Show yourself.'

'I'm not used to taking orders.' The man laughed softly and stepped nearer. 'But I like the fight in you. My name is Napoleon Bonaparte, Emperor of France. Perhaps you've heard of me?'

CHAPTER TWENTY-ONE
COUNT CRYPTOS

'Your excellency!' Dakkar said, giving a curt nod. 'It seems that your boasts of being safe from Count Cryptos were a little premature.'

'My boasts?' Bonaparte's forehead wrinkled with confusion.

'When we met last,' Dakkar said, 'you said that you didn't need our protection from Cryptos. Your bodyguard Alfonse had just killed three men . . .'

'Alfonse!' Bonaparte spat. 'That turncoat. It was because of him that I have languished here for so many months. He betrayed me, drugged my wine. I awoke in this cell and have been here ever since.'

'Many months?' Dakkar scratched his head. 'But how is that possible? I met you only a few weeks ago . . . It is I, Prince Dakkar.'

'My boy, you are mistaken,' Bonaparte said firmly. 'We have never met before. I would remember you!'

'Well, I have met you before, your excellency,' Dakkar said. He explained about their encounter, carefully avoiding any mention of the *Nautilus* or giant sharks.

Bonaparte sat absorbing his words, and after a while he lifted his head and stared at Dakkar.

'It all sounds incredible,' Bonaparte said, stroking his chin. 'The only explanation can be that you met somebody masquerading as me.'

'The man I met was an impostor?' Dakkar said, raising his eyebrows.

Napoleon gave a tired smile. 'Very possibly,' he said. 'During my time in power, I employed many doubles – impersonators, men who could take my place in dangerous situations. Some of them just held a passing resemblance to me. They would ride through the crowds quickly and the people would be cheered by my presence. Others would look like me from a distance, on a balcony or a fortress wall, addressing the people. One or two looked like my twin brother and spoke like me – maybe even thought like me. I never suspected one would overthrow me.'

'Oginski said something about how you . . . he'd changed,' Dakkar said, nodding slowly. 'I didn't think anything of it at the time. Why would someone do that though?'

Napoleon puffed out his chest. 'The people will rise up behind Napoleon,' he said, lifting his chin. 'My armies will follow him and rebuild an empire.' His shoulders sagged. 'Only it won't be me. Cryptos will control the impostor. The double will be his puppet and Cryptos will control all of Europe.'

'Very astute!' said a voice from the doorway.

Dakkar turned to see a tall man, burly and dressed in tight-fitting breeches, knee-high boots and a loose cotton shirt. There was no mistaking that he was an Oginski. He had the same dark, brooding eyes and curly hair, and yet he seemed much younger than Dakkar's Oginski.

'Count Cryptos?' Dakkar said, narrowing his eyes at the man.

'Stefan Oginski will do just fine,' the man said with a faint smile. 'I prefer to think that the name Cryptos describes my organisation rather than myself.'

'Your brother revelled in the name,' Dakkar said coldly. 'Before he died.'

'I am not my brother Kazmer,' Stefan said, quiet menace in his voice. 'Nor am I my elder brother Franciszek. The man you so revered.'

'You speak as if he's dead,' Bonaparte said.

'By all accounts he is,' Stefan murmured, fixing Dakkar with a cold stare. 'I made sure of that. Did you like the sharks? I had Alfonse release them from their cage once you thought you had escaped in that damned submersible of yours.'

'You lie!' Dakkar yelled, lunging at Stefan, who stepped aside, swatting at Dakkar with the back of his hand. Dakkar stumbled back into Bonaparte, who caught and steadied him.

'Careful, mon ami,' he said. 'Save your anger for when you most need it.'

'He's not dead,' Dakkar muttered, meeting Stefan's gaze. 'But I won't forget what you did to Gog and his tribe.'

'They had served their purpose and refused to work for me.' Stefan shrugged. 'They are barely above the animals.'

'Gog has more humanity in his little finger than you have in your whole body,' Dakkar said through gritted teeth.

'My brother has mentored you poorly,' Stefan said, raising his eyebrows. 'Come, let me show you around so you can see what you're up against. Georgia pleads well for you. I fear you may shake her resolve to support us.'

'Why would I want a tour?' Dakkar spat.

Stefan shrugged. 'It will prolong your life. I can always have you shot here and now if you prefer,' he said, nodding to the two guards who stood behind him in the passage.

Dakkar glanced at Bonaparte, who shrugged and nodded as if to say, '*What have you got to lose?*'

Stefan led Dakkar out of the cell and into the passage. The two guards from before flanked Dakkar, clutching their rifles warily. They passed cell doors on either side of them. Dakkar wrinkled his nose. A foul smell of rotten meat and excrement filled the corridor. The smell grew stronger as the passage opened into a large room.

In the dim light, Dakkar could barely make out any detail. Gradually as his eyes became accustomed to the gloom, he made out the edges of a pit that filled the centre of the room. A narrow walkway of stone ran round the edges of the pit but there were no rails to prevent them from tumbling over. Stakes dotted the sides of the pit and Dakkar shuddered as he realised that each wooden pole had a human skull sitting on its top. Deep below them, Dakkar heard hissing and snapping. The stink from the darkness nearly knocked Dakkar off his feet.

'My death pit. Full of lizards from the jungle,' Stefan said. He stopped and ran a finger over one of the skulls. 'Some of Kazmer's men managed to escape when you destroyed his island.' He stopped and held the skull close to Dakkar. 'They brought news of his demise.'

'You killed them?' Dakkar gasped, staring into the skull's empty eye sockets.

'I detest failure,' Stefan said, planting the skull back on the pole. 'It is infectious. My men know not to come back to me if they have failed a mission. They succeed or die trying.'

A flight of stairs led them to a cleaner, busier corridor. Men marched past, saluting Stefan. Light flooded in through the tall windows, dazzling Dakkar at first. He looked out over a wide space dotted with huts and buildings. A line of soldiers mounted on lizards paraded across a drill square in formation, wheeling and turning as the lead rider barked commands.

'Can you imagine the horror of the British, the Dutch and the Prussian soldiers when they encounter my lizard cavalry?' Stefan said, his voice hoarse with excitement. 'They'll tear any conventional army to pieces.'

'You intend to fight the armies of Europe?' Dakkar said. 'I thought Cryptos liked to be unknown and mysterious.'

'Unknown until the moment we strike! It will be Napoleon's armies that do the bulk of the fighting, but when the time is right my lizard legions will be unleashed,' Stefan said, grinning. 'The time and place has been decided. With France victorious and under our control, the rest of the continent will fall.'

'And then what?' Dakkar said, watching a gigantic lizard with a body bigger than an elephant and a huge long neck thunder past, dragging a load of sawn logs behind it. 'You will rule in the place of kings?'

'I will revenge myself on those who destroyed my inheritance and my family,' Stefan said, gripping Dakkar's shoulder with whitened knuckles. 'I will plunge the nations of Europe into anarchy and carve a new empire for Cryptos from the ruins.' Dakkar remembered the story of the Brothers Oginski. They were noblemen who had vied for the affections of the beautiful peasant girl Celina. They each went on a quest in order to decide who was worthy of her hand. But when they returned, they found their land plundered by Russian soldiers, their parents slain and Celina gone. In their grief they pledged vengeance on the tsar and, ultimately, on all empires of the world.

The tower shook a little and the deep rumbling sound echoed through the tunnels. Dakkar looked at the stone walls nervously.

'Don't worry, Prince Dakkar,' Stefan said, snapping out of his manic stare and laughing. 'What you hear is the harnessed power of the earth itself. Come.'

He led Dakkar through another set of doors and into a metal cage with a thick cork mat. *This is like the cage we came down here in*, Dakkar observed. It was almost identical – metal runners up the side of the shaft wall housed greased wheels.

'I call this my Ascender Cage,' the count said, grinning.

He turned a red wheel that stuck out of a copper pipe. Steam hissed beneath them and then, suddenly, Dakkar's stomach lurched. He nearly fell over as the cage shot upward.

'We are powered by pressured steam,' Stefan shouted above the clatter of the cage and the hiss of vapour. 'It's heated by the earth itself – no coal needed. Mother Nature provides the heat and the water.'

Dakkar gripped the side of the cage as it flew past floor after floor. Nausea twisted his gut and he stared down at his feet.

Stefan had closed his eyes, and stood with his hands clasped in front of him.

Seizing his chance, Dakkar leapt forward and snagged the lever down, making the cage stop with a jerk. The count gave a shout but Dakkar wrenched the cage door open and ran out into a dark passage.

Dakkar's feet slapped on the stone floor and he panted for breath. The sudden stop had made him feel sick and running didn't help. The corridor curved round the outside of the tower. Spotting a door, Dakkar swung it open and dived through.

The heat hit Dakkar first, a dry warmth that enveloped

him. He found himself in a dimly lit, musty-smelling room lined with shelves. Straw filled each shelf and row upon row of eggs rested on the straw. Large eggs.

'You can't hide up here for long,' Stefan called down the passage.

Dakkar pressed his ear to the door. He could hear the count's footsteps coming closer, then another noise behind him caught his attention. A sharp crack.

He turned to face the rows of eggs. His heart pounded as, to his horror, a jagged line appeared in the shell of the egg directly in front of him. Fascinated but wary, Dakkar backed away until he bumped into the door. A claw picked at the splintering shell from inside the egg. Then another, ripping frantically at the brittle casing.

With a yell, Dakkar covered his head with his arms as the egg exploded and the thing inside burst out, throwing itself at him.

CHAPTER TWENTY-TWO
GWEEK

Something fluttered and flapped around Dakkar's head and then moved away to the shelf close to him. Peering between his fingers, Dakkar could see what looked like a miniature Gacheela, preening itself with its long beak. It stretched its wings and gave them a flap.

Dakkar watched warily. The creature was a perfect copy of the huge monster that had nearly killed him at the caves. He edged forward. It fluttered its wings, sending Dakkar scurrying back two paces. *It's so smooth. It looks harmless.*

'Hello there,' he said in a gentle voice.

The creature made a tiny squeak and turned its head to fix a beady eye on Dakkar. A long crest sprouted from the back of its head. Dakkar extended a finger and the lizard hopped forward.

Swallowing hard, Dakkar resisted the urge to pull his finger back as the creature crept clumsily towards him.

'Don't be afraid,' Dakkar whispered, and made some gentle clicking noises.

'Gweek!' squeaked the lizard, and launched itself forward.

Dakkar gave a cry as it landed on his head. Tiny claws scratched his scalp and tangled in his hair and he swatted at the thing.

'Gweek!' it croaked again, and landed on his shoulder.

Dakkar raised his fist, his left eye closed and his head tilted away from the beast, expecting it to peck at his face. He froze and gradually opened his eye. The creature trembled on Dakkar's shoulder.

Slowly, Dakkar lowered his hand to the lizard and it hopped on to his thumb. Then, with a flap and a bounce, it jumped on to his head again. Its claws prickled Dakkar's scalp and he laughed as it ran its beak-like jaw through his hair.

'Gweek,' it said, and flapped its wings.

'Gweek,' Dakkar repeated. 'As good a name as any. I call you Gweek then.'

The door swung open and Stefan peered in. 'That was a foolish thing to do,' he said. 'Ah, I see you've found our incubation room. The reptile has bonded with you.'

'Bonded?' Dakkar said, narrowing his eyes at the count.

'The lizard will bond with the first creature it sees after hatching. This is how our riders control their beasts. At first we used wild lizards and tried to break them like horses. It worked to a degree but when the giants showed us how to create the bond we realised it was a much better way to control them.'

'Ruling through fear and cruelty rarely works,' Dakkar said, hardening his face. 'But then I suppose you wouldn't understand that.'

'Your flying pet will follow you unto death now,' the count said, ignoring Dakkar's jibe and pulling a pistol from his belt. 'He will grow no bigger than he is now. We use them for messages as they have an uncanny knack of finding their masters. It is quite magical. Come, I have one more thing to show you. Please don't try to run away again or I will shoot you where you stand.'

Dakkar followed the count back into the passageway, Gweek fluttering behind them.

'Can you feel the slightest sensation of movement?' Stefan said.

Dakkar nodded. 'It feels as if the tower is swaying,' he said, trying not to show his alarm.

'It is,' the count said, giving a grin. 'Even though it was built by giants, at this height the structure moves in the breeze.'

'Why does it have to be so high?' Dakkar said, scowling at Stefan. 'To match your soaring ego?'

'Oh! Very good, my princeling!' The count laughed, clapping his hands. 'A trip to the very top of the tower will reveal all.'

Dakkar looked out of the window and down on the ranks of riders massing below. They looked tiny. The count stopped by the Ascender Cage again.

'My armies gather,' Stefan said, grinning and rubbing his hands. 'The first squadrons will soon be on the surface awaiting my orders. And I will choose the right moment!' He opened the door to the cage and stepped in.

Dakkar followed reluctantly. The cage sped upward, making Dakkar's head swirl. He shivered as the air cooled.

'The tower goes through the gas cloud here,' the count explained. 'Most of the upper tower is empty apart from the pipes and mechanisms that power the lifts. The cloud is quite poisonous. Many of my workers died building this section.'

'Slaves, you mean,' Dakkar said, watching the walls flash by.

Stefan pursed his lips and slammed the stop lever down so that the cage rattled to an abrupt halt. Dakkar stumbled forward against the metalwork, making Gweek squawk with alarm.

'Out here,' the count murmured, opening the door. 'We have reached the top.'

Dakkar's eyes widened as he stared through the door. A brisk wind plucked at Dakkar's hair even inside the cage. The flat top of the tower stretched around for hundreds of feet in all directions. No fence or railing marked the edge. Ranks of guards stood on this flat rooftop with their muzzled lizards at their sides. Row upon row stood waiting to enter another, larger cage at the end of the flat roof of the tower. This cage led up into solid rock.

'That is the bedrock of the upper world – our ceiling down here, hidden by cloud,' Stefan said, dragging Dakkar out of the cage by the arm. 'A final Ascender Cage takes them up to the surface. I believe you're familiar with the Mole Machines that were developed by my late brother – we used them to dig the tunnel to the surface.'

Two cylindrical machines with huge pointed drills at their noses stood to one side of the lines of cavalry. Dakkar's head spun; the sheer height made his stomach rise to his throat. The wind whipped at his hair and buffeted his ears. The count pulled him to the edge of the tower. Dakkar swallowed hard and tried to control his breathing.

'Look around you,' the count shouted above the wind. 'I already rule this inner world. I would have killed you when I found you unconscious in my pits but Georgia said you had potential. I'm giving you one chance.'

'You want me to join you?' Dakkar shouted back.

'I would never make the same mistake my brother made,' the count said, pushing his thick, black hair from his face. 'You would be guarded night and day. The men who watched you would have orders to kill you at the slightest suspicion. But, yes, I see something in you – a spark of genius and energy that it would be a shame to snuff out.'

'I'd never join you,' Dakkar spat. 'I'd rather be dead.'

'As you wish,' Stefan said with a shrug.

Dakkar felt the man's large hand hit his chest and then the world spun. Dakkar's stomach lurched. He found himself falling backward, looking at his feet and beyond that the count's leering face as it vanished above him.

He pushed me off, Dakkar thought, not quite believing it. *He just pushed me off the tower!*

Time slowed down. Dakkar watched the stone blocks of the wall pass him by. He picked out every detail despite the real speed at which they flew past. Moss filled the crevices between each block; cracks crept across some stones, while others were smooth and unblemished. The air roared in Dakkar's ears and pulled at his hair and clothes. He panted, desperately catching breaths of air as he fell. Dakkar was dimly aware of Gweek's frantic squeaks and cries. The little creature flapped around him, trying to rest on his twisting and turning body. Below Dakkar, the bank of cloud grew closer, lightning flashing inside its rolling mass.

A dark shadow passed underneath Dakkar, making him blink. Gweek's cries grew shriller as they tumbled on. Dakkar squinted, trying to see as the rushing wind pressed at his eyeballs. Gweek circled again and then a deafening cry cut above the howl of the air.

Dakkar stared at the enormous creature. It resembled the Gacheela in shape, with its pointed head and stunted body. But its wings stretched on forever, the leathery membranes between its body and bony arms rippling like the sails of a galleon. This beast was enormous. It swooped around, responding to Gweek's alarmed cries. Its wing tip grazed Dakkar's shoulder and then it wheeled suddenly, as if searching for Gweek. It brought itself under Dakkar and stabbed at him with its long beak, prodding and probing for the little flying lizard. *It heard Gweek's cries and thought it was food!* Dakkar realised.

Not wasting another second, Dakkar arched his back and straightened his body into a dive, trying to increase the speed of his descent. He crashed into the giant Gacheela, gripping his arms around its neck and his legs around its body. Gasping and panting, Dakkar ignored the bristly skin that rubbed against him like sandpaper. The monster tried to peck at him but its long head prevented it from hitting him with any force. It twirled, trying to shake him off, but Dakkar gripped tightly. All this time Gweek clung to his jacket and squawked in panic.

Dakkar felt his scalp prickle and realised that they had lost height. Clearly the beast didn't have the strength to support them both. Dakkar took a deep breath, holding it as the cloud grew thicker.

The giant Gacheela flapped its wings but still couldn't shake Dakkar loose. As it struggled to free itself, the creature plunged deeper into the cloud bank. Dakkar squeezed his eyes shut. His skin stung as if a thousand needles had been stuck into it. The static charge that the clouds generated made his hair stand on end. His breath tightened in his chest. *If I breathe in now, the cloud will burn me inside.*

They were descending fast now. Gweek had somehow crept on to Dakkar's chest and inside his jacket. It croaked feebly. Even the giant flying reptile seemed weakened by the cloud and its heavy load. It spread its wings and tried to glide down through the cloud. Dakkar's lungs felt as if they would burst. His head throbbed and his grip weakened.

Then Dakkar saw the green of the jungle through the thinning mist. It grew clearer and he let out a huge gasp, drawing in fresh air. The Gacheela seemed to awaken too, swooping down towards the trees and then beyond to the sea.

The jungle became a green blur as they whipped across the treetops, then it vanished to be replaced with steel-grey water. Spray and salt water slapped Dakkar's face as once more he fought for breath. He thought about letting go but the impact at this speed would break every bone in his body. The Gacheela was taking him far out to sea!

CHAPTER TWENTY-THREE
DEAD MAN WALKING

Clinging tightly to the underside of the Gacheela, Dakkar tried to think quickly. Every second took him further and further out to sea. He looked across the slate-grey water to the horizon. He could see the land curving round the edges of this huge expanse of water. In the far distance, massive water spouts curled up into the clouds. *Admiring the scenery isn't going to help me now!* he thought, wondering what he could do to save himself.

If he tried to pull the creature down, he would be plunged into the depths with no way of getting back. The swell of the waves rolled a few feet away from him, hissing and snapping at his back like a wild animal eager to pull him in and devour him. Gweek's cries of alarm had grown louder since they had left the cloud.

I've got to turn this beast round, he thought, gritting his teeth against the ache in his arms and legs. He reached out and shifted his weight slightly to the left of the

Gacheela, bringing a flurry of squawks and attempted pecks. The beast was gliding over the waves rather than flapping now and so, gradually, Dakkar's weight began to ease it into a slow arc. The Gacheela quietened and kept low to the waves.

Eventually, they faced land again. By dangling his head down, Dakkar could see the upside-down strip of jungle on the horizon with the tower poking up into the clouds. The reptile tried to turn but Dakkar eased his weight over, making a crooked line back for shore. Each time the Gacheela changed direction, Dakkar swung himself to the left or right, forcing it to hold the right course.

Soon, Dakkar risked dangling down again and could see individual trees dotting the shoreline. A colossal shadow just under the surface killed the whoop of joy in his throat. With a yelp, Dakkar dragged himself up on to the side of the Gacheela's body, dragging it round and making it wheel back towards the seas. It snapped at him, its toothed beak snagging on his ragged jacket.

Then the sea erupted. A huge whale-like creature exploded from the depths below. The smell of the sea, rotten fish and seaweed engulfed them. Dakkar saw enormous, gaping jaws, a red mouth, row upon row of sharp ivory teeth, before he found himself flying unaided across the waves. Gweek croaked and squealed as they skipped across the water like a stone skimmed by a giant child. The tiny flying reptile fluttered up off Dakkar and squeaked its complaint above him. Cold water soaked into Dakkar's thick woollen jacket, making him gasp and pulling him down.

He caught a last glimpse of the enormous whale, the giant Gacheela crumpled in its jaws as it boomed back into the water behind him. Then a massive wave from the creature's re-entry into the sea swelled up towards them.

Turning on his stomach, Dakkar began to thrash at the water in a vain attempt to outswim the wave, but he felt himself lifted and powered along. Looking up, he saw how incredibly close the shoreline actually was. Then the wave broke, turning him head over feet. Water flooded his nose and mouth. A bubbling roar filled his ears and he found himself plunged deep beneath the surge into calmer waters below.

Dakkar opened his eyes. Ever since Oginski had taken him and introduced him to the sea, Dakkar had found he could see well underwater. Now he stared at the rocky bed below him, teeming with strange fish. Some had long filaments waving from their heads, others had pronounced lower jaws and legions of needle-sharp teeth. Strange worms wriggled among the vivid red seaweed and the black, volcanic rock. Here, too, creatures preyed upon each other with an insatiable hunger.

Glancing round for any larger fish, Dakkar kicked his way to the surface, gasping for breath as he hit the cool air. Gweek fluttered above him, croaking.

'I'm fine, thanks,' Dakkar panted with a grin. 'So glad you were worried about my safety,' he added as the tiny reptile landed on his head and rested its wings.

Dakkar surged forward, cutting through the water with a powerful stroke, and soon his feet found the sandy seabed. Within a few minutes, he threw himself on to the beach that skirted the sea. The jungle stood a few paces away but even from here he could see the tower rising upward, sheer and menacing.

The one advantage I have now is that Cryptos thinks I'm dead, he thought, chewing his lip.

He picked himself up from the sand and trudged to the fringes of the jungle, scanning this way and that for any would-be predators. Gweek had fallen silent, content to sit on his shoulder and preen his scaly skin with his sharp beak.

The same eerie quiet hung over this part of the jungle. A few smaller lizards skittered up tree trunks and the odd bird-like creature hopped above Dakkar in the branches but the rest of the wildlife kept to the deeper forest.

Dakkar's foot crunched against something and he leapt back, stifling a yell. His foot had sunk into the ribcage of a human skeleton. Pulling a face, he glanced around. Several bodies had lain here, all dressed in Cryptos uniforms, but now only bleached bone and filthy fabric remained. They had been shot in the head, judging by the holes broken in the skulls. *Maybe this was one of Cryptos's own executions*, Dakkar thought.

The uniforms looked intact. Dakkar pursed his lips then pulled at one of the jackets. The skeleton fell apart, desiccated by the sun. He shook the jacket, spluttering in the disgusting dust cloud that enveloped him. Gweek gave a squawk and fluttered up to the lowest branches.

It might just fit me, he thought. *And if I can clean it up I might just trick my way back into the tower.*

Washing the uniform jacket in the salty seawater seemed to clear the soil and other stains from it quite effectively. Dakkar scrambled up a conifer and hung it on a branch to dry. He lay back in the crook of the branch, his back against the trunk, and stared at the tower.

I wonder what's happened to Mary, he thought. *And what is Georgia up to? If she really had gone over to Cryptos, then she would have given Stefan the* Liberty.

Even the crowding thoughts couldn't stop sleep from creeping up on him. A gentle breeze from the sea sighed through the needles of the tree, making it sway gently to the rhythm of the waves. Soon he was dreaming that he lay on the deck of the *Nautilus* with the sun warming his face.

Dakkar woke with a start. Something scratched at his cheek. He waved his hand in the air and rubbed his eyes simultaneously, causing him to overbalance. The ground loomed up at him for a moment and he only just managed to stop himself from falling.

Gweek flapped around his head, fussing and croaking at him. Dakkar shook himself. *How long have I been asleep?* he thought. It was so difficult to tell in this nightless world.

He extended his arm and Gweek settled on to it. Dakkar smiled and tickled its neck. The skin felt surprisingly soft, like kid leather.

'You're still here?' he said, grinning at Gweek.

Dakkar checked the guard's jacket, smiling when he realised how dry it was. The exposure to the salt water and the sea breeze had shrunk the fabric so that it fitted him quite snugly. His trousers looked rather ragged but with the tricorne hat he spied in the undergrowth pulled down low on his brow he might just get away with it.

Checking the ground for any concealed pits, Dakkar inched his way to the edge of the jungle and watched. A few squadrons of riders appeared, dragging giants tied at the wrists. One came close to the fringes of the forest, their prisoners stumbling – and flinching at the lashes they received as a result. The leader of the group had a round, ruddy face and one blind, milky eye.

'Get them moving!' he bellowed at the men, who whipped and prodded the poor giants. 'I've been out of the tower too long. I need some beer!'

At the very rear of the group, a four-legged reptile with a strange beak and a frilled plate round its head pulled a small cart. The reptile slowed to a stop and its driver jumped off the cart to push the beast's rump as if he could move it.

Dakkar stuffed Gweek under his tricone hat, pulled it down and ran from the bushes to join the breathless driver, who nodded gratefully.

'Thank 'ee,' said the driver. 'Where did you spring from?'

'Was fixin' some pit traps in the forest,' Dakkar lied, lowering his voice. 'I saw you needed help.'

'That's the truth,' the driver spat. 'This bloomin' beast 'as been playin' up all day!'

Dakkar noticed the strange spiky fruit that comprised the cart's load. They reminded him of pineapples but they were black and had much broader leaves. He winked at the driver and pulled one from the pile.

'Maybe we can bribe him,' Dakkar said, moving to the front of the beast.

'They're not for animals,' the driver said, but then he noticed that the reptile was moving again as Dakkar held it a few inches ahead.

'I won't tell if you don't.' Dakkar grinned and handed the pineapple to the driver, who took over leading the creature.

Dakkar followed behind the cart, hidden from the view of the others by the pile of fruit and the bulk of the struggling giants. He desperately wanted to free them but knew only too well that in doing so he would give himself away. He had to play along and get inside the stockade. Only then could he help.

The stockade walls drew nearer and Dakkar's heart thumped in his chest. He prayed that Gweek would keep still and silent under his hat.

The bleached, barren plain they crossed to get to the tower reminded Dakkar of a desert, except now and then they passed a gurgling hole in the earth which steamed and boiled.

As they drew closer, Dakkar could see how crude the wall was. Tree trunks had been sharpened and buried into the ground to form the tall barrier. A double gate swung open to allow the party through. Two black-clad guards stood, rifles in the crook of their arms, watching everything.

A fruit tumbled from the pile and Dakkar stooped to pick it up as the cart approached the gates.

'Stop,' said the nearest guard as the cart rolled on, exposing Dakkar. The guard levelled his rifle and stared at Dakkar.

He'd been caught.

CHAPTER TWENTY-FOUR
CAUGHT

Dakkar froze, the sweat trickling down his back. He raised his hands, the fruit still in one, trying to decide if it felt heavy enough to use as a weapon.

'You missed one,' the guard said, laughing and pointing at another fruit on the ground at his feet. 'Don't waste any! Them pineapple things are about the tastiest dish in these parts.'

'Yeah.' The guard's partner sauntered over and poked the fruit with the toe of his boot. 'I'll have one o' them over fried reptile any day!'

'Maybe you might want to rescue that one when I've passed,' Dakkar said, keeping his head down. 'Nobody will know.'

The guards looked at each other and then at the fruit he held.

'You might sort of drop that one too,' the first guard said. 'By accident.'

The fruit in Dakkar's hand thumped to the ground
and he strode in through the gates as the two guards
bent to pick the fruit up. He allowed himself a smile at
the thought that he'd just wandered through Cryptos's
front gates without any real problem. Dakkar lifted his
hat slightly and allowed Gweek to flutter out and land
on his shoulder.

Buildings and drill squares filled up the space between
the stockade and the tower walls. A series of large iron
cages held reptiles that hissed and snapped at each other
through the bars. A corral fenced in more docile herbiv-
orous creatures the size of rhinos but with bony armour
plating and many horns. Men hurried about, carrying
bales of hay or pushing barrows of provisions. Carts
loaded with barrels trundled past and, in the bustle,
Dakkar went unnoticed.

Grabbing an empty basket, Dakkar began walking
around the base of the tower, looking for a sign of
weakness, anything he could use to his advantage. The
blocks of stone that supported the tower stood as tall as
Dakkar. He could imagine the giants heaving them
into position, friendly and cooperative at first, helping
their friend Stefan. Then, gradually, as his demands
grew they would have left only to be dragged back as
slaves. The tower's walls stretched ahead of him; its
foundations had to be broad and deep, he guessed, to
support such a height.

Barred windows carved out of the stone appeared in
the walls at ground level. Dakkar recognised them as

the windows to the cells in which he had met Bonaparte. He strolled past them, swinging his basket casually and glancing down through the bars of each window as he went.

Glum faces gazed up, many of them giants huddled together. Women and children stared with hopeless expressions, dirt smearing their faces. In other cells, savage reptiles leapt up and bit at the bars, hissing and making Dakkar jump back. Finally, he came to a quiet cell, with a silent figure sitting in the corner. Dakkar knelt down close to the bars, pretending to tie his shoelace. Gweek gave a squawk of protest and fluttered on to Dakkar's head.

'Your excellency?' Dakkar hissed. 'Is it you? Can you speak to me?'

'Dakkar?' Bonaparte's pale face appeared at the window. 'I thought you were dead!'

'Nearly,' Dakkar whispered. 'I haven't much time. The count is moving his reptile cavalry to the surface.'

'These are the preparations for battle,' Bonaparte said, craning his neck and watching the men hurrying about behind Dakkar. 'Cryptos will want a confrontation with all the world powers, somewhere he can face the massed armies of Europe and their generals and so annihilate them.'

'We can stop him before that happens,' Dakkar said, 'if I can destroy the top of the tower and cut off their supply chain.'

'I fear too many of his troops may be up there already,'

Napoleon said with a sigh. Then a grin spread slowly across his face. 'I suppose a little chaos might slow things down.'

'I'll try to sneak in and free you –' Dakkar began, but Bonaparte held up a hand.

'No,' he said. 'First you need a distraction. Many of the men are absorbed in their duties. Over there,' Napoleon said, pointing a finger beyond Dakkar to a square stone building, 'that is where they store their gunpowder and weapons. I have watched them for many days. They are taking barrels of explosive up to the top of the tower.'

'If I blow that storehouse up they'll be busy dealing with that,' Dakkar said. 'I can get in and rescue you.'

'It may be worth a try,' Napoleon said. He tugged at the bars as if he could pull them apart and climb out. 'I'll stay here.' He gave a wry smile. 'Bon chance, mon ami!'

Dakkar jumped up and marched over to the square stone building that stood at the fringe of the stockade. It had no windows and only one door. Solid stone slabs covered the top of the building, making it look like some ancient tomb. Clearly any explosion inside the building would be easily contained. Dakkar cursed under his breath.

'Don't just stand there, lad,' snapped a curt voice behind him. 'Grab a barrel if you've got time to idle away!'

Gweek gave a startled croak and Dakkar spun round to see the ruddy-faced guard who had led the giants

into the tower before. He shoved a small barrel of powder into Dakkar's open arms, making him stagger
backward.

'Here's me just come off a two-day patrol. No time for
a rest,' the man muttered, stamping off towards the tower
wall. 'Every man to his post.'

The man spat on the ground and continued grumbling, but Dakkar wasn't listening any more. He watched
as they joined a procession of men who stacked barrel
after barrel into an Ascender Cage. This one ran up the
outside of the tower and was a completely enclosed box
made of copper. Rails set into a deep recess ran up the
side of the tower.

'Does that go up to the very top?' Dakkar gasped in
wonder.

'Course it does, and the count is up there gettin' belly-
ache because we've fallen behind with sendin' the powder
up, so get movin'!' the grumpy, red-faced guard barked at
him.

They stacked their barrels and Dakkar sprinted back
to the huge metal door of the powder store, where a
guard and a tall, thin man with a bundle of papers
stood arguing.

'I don't know where we're up to,' the thin man said,
throwing his hands up and dropping half the papers. 'Your
men are just grabbing anything and stuffing it into the
ascender.'

'I'll stuff you in the ascender in a min—' the burly guard
snapped.

'Sorry to interrupt, sirs,' Dakkar panted, pretending to be out of breath. 'The count wants to know where the fuses are.'

'Fuses?' the thin man said, going pale and flicking through his sheets. 'But I thought we . . .'

'Ten-minute fuses,' Dakkar said. He widened his eyes. 'Please, sir, have pity. Don't send me back without them. The count, he's in a proper rage . . .'

'Is he?' The thin man went even paler and swallowed hard. 'Come with me.'

Dakkar followed the man into the cool shadows of the storehouse. Their footsteps echoed in what was essentially a man-made cave, a huge hall built to store weapons. Even half emptied the place looked crowded with barrels cluttering the floor, shelves stacked with sacks and racks full of rifles.

The man stopped at a chest of drawers and pulled open a drawer with a number *10* on it. He emptied the contents into Dakkar's hands.

'Thank you,' Dakkar said, scarcely believing his luck. He turned to leave.

'Wait!' the man said.

Dakkar's stomach lurched. He turned to face the man.

'You may as well take some tinderboxes too,' the man said. 'Maybe the count will be lenient on us all if he thinks we've used our initiative.'

'I'm sure he will, sir,' Dakkar said, smiling and pocketing the boxes.

'Go on, then. Run, lad,' the thin man said, clapping

his hands. 'We wouldn't want to upset the count, would we?'

'No, sir,' Dakkar said, grinning as he turned his back on the thin man.

Dakkar gripped the fuses and ran back to the ascender, which was virtually full now.

'I'll take her up,' Dakkar shouted.

The guard holding the ascender doors, who looked rather like a gorilla in uniform, jutted his hairy chin. 'Says who?' he murmured, frowning with deep, bushy eyebrows.

'I'm smaller than you,' Dakkar said. 'We can fit another barrel in. The count will be astounded by your quick thinking.'

'He will?' the gorilla guard said, giving a brown-toothed grin.

'He'll be totally amazed,' Dakkar said, pushing his way into the cage and edging the guard out.

'Well, if you think so,' the gorilla said.

'Here, hold this,' Dakkar said, snatching Gweek out of the air and stuffing it into the gorilla's huge hand.

'Oh, righto,' the gorilla said, frowning at the tiny flying reptile that pecked at his thumb. 'Be sure to let him know it was my idea!'

'Certain to, sir.' Dakkar gave an exaggerated salute, implying immediate promotion.

The gorilla puffed his chest out, saluted back and clanged the doors shut.

A half-light filled the box of the ascender. Dakkar knew they used copper as it was hard to strike a spark on and thus safe for transporting explosives. Without waiting, he pulled the bungs out of two barrels of powder then he took the fuse and twisted it into the holes. Dakkar fumbled with the lid of the tinderbox. *What if I strike the spark and blow myself to pieces?*

'Are you all right in there?' the gorilla outside called, banging on the door.

'I can't find the handle,' Dakkar lied as he struck a spark into the soft linen fibre in the tinderbox. A small flame flickered into life. 'Left or right?'

The gorilla paused for a moment. 'It's on the side – left, I think.'

Dakkar pushed the fuse wire into the flame and it hissed into life.

'Got it!' Dakkar yelled back, slamming the ascender's lever up.

The cage rattled into life and Dakkar stayed low, throwing himself forward. The cage doors burst open and Dakkar tumbled out at the gorilla's feet. The gorilla stared down at him, mouth open. Gweek wriggled from his grasp and fluttered out of reach, screeching indignantly.

'What're you doin' there?' the gorilla spluttered. 'Who'll stop the cage at the top?'

'Oh, it'll stop all right,' Dakkar said, standing up and dusting himself down. 'You keep looking up there and you'll see.'

The gorilla lifted his head, jaw still gaping.

Dakkar gave a grin and turned round to leave.

'Not so fast, Prince Dakkar,' a familiar voice called. Count Stefan Oginski stood, flanked by Georgia and Mary Anning. 'I thought I'd killed you already but this time I will make certain of it.'

CHAPTER TWENTY-FIVE
CHAOS REIGNS

The gorilla shoved Dakkar against the cold stone wall of the tower. The count strode up to Dakkar, snatching a rifle from a nearby guard. Several more guards formed a semicircle around Dakkar, their guns drawn. Gweek flew above Dakkar's head in confusion.

'I don't know how you survived that fall,' the count said through gritted teeth, 'but this time I'm going to shoot you myself.'

Dakkar looked from Georgia to Mary. 'So you're going to watch him kill me?'

'I've explained to Mary how it is,' Georgia said carefully. 'You had a chance but you threw it away.'

'*He* threw *me* off the tower!' Dakkar snapped. 'I hardly had much of a chance.'

'You could have joined me,' the count said. He clicked back the lock on the rifle and strode a few paces away.

'Wait!' Georgia shouted. 'We need to know what he's done, surely.'

'He was up to no good in that ascender,' Mary added. She pointed to the gorilla. 'Ask 'im.'

'He didn't even know where the lever was to start the thing,' scoffed the gorilla. Then he frowned. 'He did jump out smartish though!'

The count raised the rifle and pointed it at Dakkar, then turned it on the gorilla and fired.

The gorilla yelped and stumbled backward, clutching his ear. 'Thanks, your greatness,' he whimpered. 'I'll wear that scar with pride.'

'I was aiming for your nose,' the count said, slapping the empty rifle into Mary's hand. Another guard ran up with a freshly loaded one. 'But next time maybe you'll remember not to let total strangers do your job for you.' He raised the rifle again. 'Now, Prince Dakkar, suppose you tell me what it was you were up to in that ascender.'

'You'll know soon enough,' Dakkar said, giving a tight smile. 'You can kill me if you like but your game is over.'

'Well, if I have your permission.' The count grinned and settled the stock of the rifle into his shoulder.

Georgia leapt forward, landing a fist square on the count's jaw, while Mary grabbed his rifle. The gun went off but a louder sound above them drowned it out completely, making everyone freeze and stare upward.

High above, the cloud layer glowed bright orange and swirled as if blown by some giant's breath. A deafening roar filled the air and the ground beneath their feet shivered.

'It's over,' Dakkar said simply.

The smouldering carcass of a reptile thudded to the ground between the count and Dakkar. Stefan stared in horror at this strange sight. Then another landed and another, crushing two guards before they could even scream. Another pounded the drill square, kicking up a fog of dust.

'It's raining reptiles,' cried the gorilla, running towards the gunpowder store with his hands over his head.

More rubble began to clatter to earth. Spars of flaming wood stabbed into the ground like giant spears. Rocks and boulders thudded down. One crashed into the cages holding the wild reptiles, killing a few but liberating many. These leapt from their prisons, pouncing on men, ripping and tearing at them.

The guards around the count began to waver, staring around at the chaos, some looking up at the sky as more debris crashed to the ground. Some fired on the reptiles. Others began to run for the stockade gate, joining an increasing crowd.

'What have you done?' the count said in a low voice.

Dust from the falling masonry billowed up in a huge fog. Screams and explosions, crashes and thuds punctuated the continuous rumbling from above. A whole section of wall thumped into the earth, taking the fence of the herbivores' corral down and panicking the beasts.

The earth shook more violently as a grey tide of horns and armour plate rumbled across the stockade towards Dakkar and the count.

'Run!' Georgia cried, grabbing Mary's hand.

Dakkar glanced at the count, uncertain what to do next.

'Don't think this is over, boy,' Stefan said with a contemptuous sneer, and ran into the mist away from the oncoming wave of reptiles.

Dakkar had no time to reply. He could see the wild eyes of the creatures, could feel the thunder of their feet through the ground. Turning on his heel, he sprinted after Mary and Georgia.

The stampede drove them on. Mary stumbled. Dakkar gasped for breath, scooping up Mary by the arm, then he and Georgia dragged her along. The reptiles' heavy tread thundered in Dakkar's ears – they were gaining on them. More rocks tumbled from above, some thumping into the startled reptiles and rolling them into a leathery pile-up. Another minute and Dakkar, Mary and Georgia would be crushed by the frantic animals. Out of the corner of his eye, Dakkar spied the main door of the tower. Smoke poured out of it. The tower guards staggered into the path of the terrified reptiles.

'Into the tower!' Dakkar shouted. 'We have to find Gog and Napoleon!'

They veered left, throwing themselves into the tower's entrance hall as the mass of rampaging creatures crashed against the wall and surged past.

For a second, they lay gasping in a heap but smoke billowed around the hall and men scurried past them. Somewhere overhead, Gweek squawked.

'I knew you were just pretending to support Cryptos,' Dakkar lied, catching his breath. 'Thank goodness!'

'I was biding my time,' Georgia replied, staggering to her feet, 'trying to figure out what he was up to and then put a stop to it, but that involved winning his trust.'

'Well, you could've just blown 'im up like Dakkar did,' Mary said, brushing her dark hair from her face.

Georgia narrowed her eyes at Mary. 'You were all for abandoning Dax when I first met you *and* you seemed quite cosy with the count.'

'Dax?' Dakkar said, pulling a face.

'Well then, you set me a poor example, didn't you?' Mary retorted.

The whole building shuddered and masonry rattled to the stone floor. Gweek flew in through the gaping door and nestled in Dakkar's jacket, hiding from the noise and chaos.

'We haven't time for bickering,' Dakkar said, grabbing Georgia's arm. 'We need to find the cells. Can you lead us to them?'

'Of course I can,' Georgia said, hurrying across the hallway to a splintered door that hung off its hinges. 'C'mon – down here.'

They clattered down some rough stone steps and into familiar passageways lined with doors. The entire corridor trembled.

'We need to check each cell and open the doors,' Dakkar said over the increasing rumble from above.

A wild-eyed guard leapt in front of them, waving a

pistol. Blood trickled down his cheek and dust coated his uniform. Dakkar spied a bunch of keys at his belt.

'Don't move,' he said, jabbing the pistol at Dakkar.

'For goodness' sake, man,' Dakkar yelled. 'We don't have time for this. Look around you – the building is collapsing. Now give me the keys and get out of here, or do you want to wait to be crushed?' Dakkar nodded up to the ceiling as more dust and mortar streamed from between the sagging roof blocks.

The man fumbled at his belt and threw the keys at Dakkar then barged past them without a backward glance.

The deep rumbling grew louder, sending Dakkar scurrying along the passage, fumbling at the lock of each door when he saw giants inside. The corridor filled with huge figures – giant men, women and children all wide-eyed with terror. Georgia herded them through the passage and up to the stairs.

Halfway down, Dakkar threw open a door and there stood Gog, arms wrapped around a giant woman and a boy. They filled the cell yet looked small and lost at the same time.

'Gog!' Dakkar yelled, and rushed forward, wrapping his arms round the giant's huge leg.

The giant's eyes brightened. 'Dakkar,' he said, his voice booming above the grumbling building. 'What is happening?'

'No time,' Dakkar said. 'We must get everyone out.'

As if to emphasise Dakkar's point, a huge block fell into the corner of the cell.

Gog hurried out into the corridor.

He gave a guttural shout down the passageway and, realising that the guards had gone, the remaining giants inside the other cells began to kick the doors down.

'My son,' Gog said, nodding to the boy who looked sullenly at Dakkar. 'And Greela,' he said, nodding to the woman.

Dakkar gave a brief smile but this wasn't the time for introductions. 'I need to find Napoleon,' he said, hurrying to the nearest closed door and pressing his face to the bars. A hiss and a swish of claws inches from his nose told him that Bonaparte wasn't in that cell.

After two more doors, Dakkar heard the Frenchman calling to him. Dakkar hurried down the corridor and stabbed the key into the lock.

The sound of grating masonry deafened him now and huge cracks appeared across the vaulted ceiling.

'Thank you, my friend,' Napoleon gasped, hurrying alongside Dakkar. 'But when I said a distraction I meant something a little less drastic!'

'I didn't think it would be so destructive,' Dakkar said, 'but it did the job.'

Gog froze in front of them and glanced back. Giants were still crawling out of the cells and a huge crowd filled the passage behind Dakkar. They looked up at the motes of dust that poured through ever-widening cracks in the stonework. The ceiling above Gog began to give way.

CHAPTER TWENTY-SIX
SACRIFICE

The thunder of falling rock above them grew more intense. Instinctively, Gog heaved his shoulders up against the ceiling, bracing it above him. He screwed his face up and gritted his teeth. For a moment the dust settled and the ceiling held.

'I can hold,' Gog said, his whole body straining. 'Go fast!'

'No, we can do something,' Dakkar said, looking from Bonaparte to Georgia to Mary, helplessly. 'There must be . . .'

'You know there isn't time, Dakkar,' Georgia said, stifling a sob.

'Go!' Gog grunted again, sweat dripping from his brow. Every muscle in his body bulged and trembled. 'You live. Hunt. Kill Stefan.'

Someone barged Dakkar aside and Gog's son hugged the giant. He stroked his father's cheek and then was hurried away by his mother, who gave Gog a final, longing look. Dakkar stood frozen, staring into Gog's pleading eyes. The tide of giants scurrying under Gog pushed Dakkar further and further up the corridor until Mary and Georgia grabbed his arms and pulled him up the steps.

Gog gave him a last despairing smile and lowered his shaggy head. With a deafening roar, the tunnel filled with smoke and dust as the ceiling collapsed. Dakkar let himself be dragged into the hallway, where rubble bounced down the staircase like a mountain stream.

The daylight dazzled Dakkar as he stumbled outside and into the wreckage of the courtyard. Gweek wrestled itself out of his jacket and fluttered above his head. Dakkar stood with Mary, Georgia, Napoleon and a growing crowd of giants staring in dazed wonder at the carnage.

Piles of masonry dotted the ground to the stockade wall. Some chunks of the tower had flattened the wall itself, scattering the huge sharp-pointed logs that had formed it. Here and there, a reptilian leg poked out of the rubble. Smoke and dust filled the air, coating their mouths and noses.

Behind them the mountain of rocks that had once been the tower sat smouldering, bits and pieces still thumping to the ground or rattling down its steep sides. A ridge of debris stretched off across the clearing and into the sea, clearly marking where the middle of the tower had fallen. Still more had punched new clearings into the thick jungle further away.

Napoleon slapped the dust from his greatcoat and

spluttered. 'We have escaped from the frying pan,' he declared, 'but I fear we have jumped into the fire.'

The fog of dust and smoke broke to reveal a rank of Cryptos guards creeping forward through the rubble. Some were armed with rifles, a few were mounted on reptiles, but Dakkar noted with grim satisfaction that the rest were on foot. They looked warily at the giants.

'I see fear in their eyes,' Dakkar said to Napoleon.

'Kill them!' cried a voice from above.

Dakkar looked up to see the count leaning from the basket of a hot-air balloon.

'Cut them down. Show them no mercy!' the count bellowed, his eyes wide with rage.

The men looked up at the count and then back at the mass of giants who flanked Dakkar and his party. One by one, the giants grabbed at snapped beams or smaller chunks of stone, testing their weight as weapons. Some pulled at the bars of the wrecked cages, straightening the bent metal into makeshift spears.

'What are you waiting for?' the count howled. 'Attack! Attaaaaack!'

But it was the giants who responded to the count's command, answering him with a deep roar and charging forward. Some hurled their newly crafted spears – Dakkar saw a reptile rider fall, pinioned to his mount as it bounded out of the ruined stockade into the river. The giants charged forward and Dakkar joined them, adding his roar to theirs. A few gunshots went off but the Cryptos Guard didn't have time to reload before the giants were upon them.

Some men turned and ran, dropping their weapons. Dakkar snatched up a rifle and turned to aim at the balloon. It had drifted higher but still offered an easy target. He squeezed the trigger.

A loud thump deafened Dakkar and the world went black for an instant. Smoke filled his mouth and nostrils and stung his eyes. Spluttering, Dakkar dropped the rifle and stumbled back. Whoever owned the rifle had loaded it in haste. The gunpowder in the pan of the rifle had ignited, making an eye-watering cloud of smoke but nothing more.

Rubbing his eyes, Dakkar staggered forward, barging into someone. His vision cleared to reveal the bald, ruddy-faced man Dakkar had met bringing the prisoners in.

'You!' the man snarled, swinging his sword down at Dakkar.

Dakkar threw up the rifle in his hands to block the blow and pushed back, sending the man tumbling over a reptile carcass. He jumped to his feet but Dakkar brought the butt of the rifle round, catching him square on the jaw. The man twirled round, blood splattering from his mouth. He landed heavily on the ground and lay still.

Around Dakkar, giants swung improvised clubs, sending Cryptos guards flying in all directions. One giant lay pinned by a reptile rider, its teeth grazing his throat. Dakkar snatched up a bar from a smashed cage in both hands and ran, screaming, at the rider. The reptile turned its head, jaws open, and the bar sank into its throat before the rider could swing his sword down on Dakkar. The reptile reared up, wrenching the bar out of Dakkar's hands and throwing the rider to the ground, where another giant fell upon him.

Dakkar hurried on, searching for a rifle. He glanced up – the balloon was growing smaller by the second, carried up on the warm breeze.

He scanned the heaving mass of giants, reptiles and men and spotted Georgia standing on a boulder with a smoking gun. He nodded and then pointed at the balloon that was getting further away. Georgia pulled out more powder, wadding and musket balls and began loading.

A gunshot echoed across the battleground and a ball zipped past Dakkar's ear. It sank into the thigh of a nearby giant, sending him crashing to the ground. The guard who had managed to reload charged forward at Dakkar. Dakkar snatched a bayonet from the fallen guard's hand and managed to swing it up to parry the man's rifle butt. Dakkar's arm numbed from wrist to elbow with the blow. Gweek swooped down, screeching and clawing at the man's face. Dakkar kicked out as the man stumbled on past him, catching him in the side of the head. The guard scrambled to his feet and drew a pistol from his belt. Dakkar froze.

Napoleon appeared behind the guard, gripping the man's pistol arm. The guard spun round and the two struggled, the pistol between them.

Dakkar ran forward and grabbed at the guard but the pistol exploded into life and Napoleon staggered back.

Around them the tumult died and the giants stood panting for breath. The only Cryptos guard still standing held the smoking pistol.

Napoleon stared in disbelief at the crimson stain spreading across the chest of his greatcoat.

The guard glanced at Dakkar and the giants, who edged closer and closer, then made a headlong sprint for the gate.

'Napoleon!' Dakkar ran forward, cradling the emperor as he fell. 'Georgia, Mary, get bandages! Quickly!'

'No, mon ami,' Napoleon said with a rattling breath. 'I am done for.'

Georgia and Mary hurried to Dakkar's side.

'We can get the shot out,' Dakkar almost shouted. 'We must be able to do something!'

'Listen carefully,' Napoleon gasped, wincing at the effort of speaking. 'You must stop the count. He will cause chaos, and France and all Europe will be doomed. Though it pains me to say it, for the good of France you must ensure that my armies are defeated.'

'Rest yourself,' Dakkar said, his voice soothing. Images of Oginski, pale and fading fast, flashed through his mind. Gog's final smile. So much death. He *could* save Napoleon – he must!

'Listen to me!' Napoleon said, his voice gravelly. 'I have been calculating while I've been here. My double on the surface knows my plan well. He will march up through France and strike the British and Dutch from near Brussels.'

'Stefan said to me that the battleground had already been chosen,' Dakkar said, frowning. 'He wants to annihilate them all.'

'He will try to take them by surprise,' Napoleon said, his breathing ragged. 'By my calculation, the tunnel he dug will have reached the surface near there.'

'If he's marching from Paris, he'll attack from the west,' Mary said.

'If it were me,' Napoleon said, gripping Dakkar's hand, 'I would use the forces I have to get behind the British, to outflank them. And that's what he'll do.'

'But how can we stop him?' Dakkar said. 'We have no armies or cavalry!'

'You have the spark of greatness in you,' Napoleon said, clasping Dakkar's fist. 'One day, men will either fear or celebrate your name. I have faith in you.'

Napoleon's hold loosened and he gave one last breath before slumping gently into Dakkar's arms.

Dakkar wept. For Gog. For Napoleon. And for Oginski, who might be dead for all he knew. *If only he were here*, Dakkar thought. *He'd know what to do.*

He glanced up to the skies. The count's hot-air balloon was a tiny speck in the far distance.

'I will stop you, Count Cryptos,' Dakkar said, holding Napoleon's cooling hand. 'I swear it.'

CHAPTER TWENTY-SEVEN
FAREWELLS AND FORGIVENESS

A haze of woodsmoke hung over the giants' camp. In the glow of the fire, men sang and passed food and drink. Gog's son sat on a huge wooden throne, glowering into the flickering flames.

Dakkar shivered. 'We're outstaying our welcome,' he said as he sat at the door of his hut, watching the remnants of the underworld tribes dancing and telling tales.

'You can't blame Gog's son for resenting us,' Georgia said, folding her arms and leaning against the hut wall next to Dakkar. 'To him, there's little difference between us and the count's men.'

'You two wearin' them ridiculous black uniforms doesn't help,' Mary said from within the hut. She sat on a makeshift stool carved from an old log. 'A girl in trousers? You'll be carted off to the asylum when we get topside again!'

'If we *ever* get topside again,' Dakkar murmured, mulling over the past few days. After Napoleon had died and the last of the Cryptos Guard had fled, somehow Dakkar had imagined a hurried chase to the surface. 'I thought we'd be there by now.'

Reality had been a little different. The giants had laid out their dead along the shore for the Gacheela to take and spent a long time pulling bodies from the rubble. The bodies of Cryptos guards were treated with customary disrespect and thrown into the bushes for the Saranda. When Dakkar had asked for a cairn of stones over Napoleon's corpse, the giants had looked at him uncomprehendingly. Without Gog to translate, communication had become more difficult even though Dakkar had begun to pick up some key words of their language.

He didn't need a translator to tell him that Gog's son was unhappy. His dark eyes scowled at Dakkar every time their paths crossed.

'He blames you for Gog's death,' Mary said one night as they all sat round a tribal fire eating scavenged fruit from the ruined storehouses.

'There was nothing Dax could do,' Georgia said, leaping to her feet.

Dakkar stayed silent, staring at the ground.

A few of Gog's original tribesmen had survived and they greeted Dakkar with smiles and even offerings of food. Dakkar got the distinct impression that they were watching out for him at least.

The giants' funeral rites took days. Some tribesmen found feathers and the bones of fallen reptiles. They paced the ruins, shaking the feathers and chanting.

'I think they're purifying the area,' Dakkar said.

'It needs it,' Georgia replied, wrinkling her nose at the stink of decay.

The rotting carcasses of reptiles littered the site, attracting small scavenger lizards and some strange flying creatures too. Gweek would flutter off from time to time and Dakkar tried not to think about what it was eating.

'Couldn't we just go and find a way home?' Mary said, as they watched the dancing shaman.

'I'm not sure I want to venture out into that jungle alone,' Georgia muttered, shading her eyes and staring across at the distant line of trees. 'There's all kinds of beasties who've run off there recently – not to mention a few Cryptos guards.'

'I'm not scared,' Mary said, folding her arms at Georgia.

'We're better off moving in a group,' Dakkar agreed, 'frustrating as it is. I'm sure we'll find a way out of here, Mary, but we've got to stick together.'

Dakkar, Georgia and Mary spent their time scavenging what they could. They found rifles, powder and ammunition, knives and swords. Mary found supplies of dried meat and tarpaulin covers. She also found some fascinating samples of fossil which Georgia wouldn't allow on the sub 'because of their weight'. Dakkar managed to make some new Sea Arrows using bits and pieces from the arsenal.

Finally, after several days, the giants were ready to move. Although they were from different tribes, they appeared to accept Gog's son as leader. Their numbers had dwindled and while Gog had mentioned at least three tribes to Dakkar, here there barely looked enough for one. Dakkar bade a sad farewell to Napoleon's grave and followed the giants as they strode across the dead plain that surrounded the now ruined tower.

Their journey back to Gog's riverbank camp had proved tense but uneventful. The majority of the giants hadn't seen anything like the *Liberty* before, and when Dakkar and Georgia uncovered it from the bushes and reeds at the side of the river, some were scared. Gog's son scowled the deepest.

Although time was hard to measure in this night-less world, Dakkar guessed that over a week had passed since the battle at the tower.

'But we're ready to leave tomorrow, aren't we?' Mary said, pulling Dakkar from his thoughts.

'It isn't just a question of jumping in the *Liberty* and speeding off, you know,' Georgia snapped. 'We need food – enough for three of us for at least several weeks. We need water. We need to know where we're going!'

'That's not my fault,' Mary said, shrugging. 'If Dakkar hadn't smashed up the nearest Ascender Cage, I'd be back in Lyme now.'

'How did you get down here, Georgia?' Dakkar said, ignoring Mary's jibe.

'Through a sea tunnel,' Georgia said. 'The beasts I tracked from Nova Scotia brought me to an island off the coast of Africa. They swam into a cave which became a tunnel. The current was strong and it sucked me right down. I thought I was going to die.'

'Oh well, never mind,' Mary muttered just loud enough for Georgia to hear. 'Better luck next time.'

Georgia jumped up. 'You button your lip,' she snarled, 'or I'll do it for you!'

'Will you two stop?' Dakkar said, sighing. 'We've got enough on our plate trying to get home.' He looked up at the boiling clouds.

But what will I find when I get up there? he thought. *Oginski dead? The count marshalling his reptile cavalry?*

The time eventually came for them to depart. Two of Gog's old warriors accompanied them through the jungle to the river where the *Liberty* lay moored. They had packed her with the black fruit, some dried meat and the craft's water barrels were full. Dakkar's Sea Arrows were stowed and ready to use.

Now Dakkar stood on the mossy riverbank, his cheeks flushed, unsure what to say. The two giants waited, giving toothy grins and nodding. Then Gog's son appeared from the undergrowth. He stared at Dakkar then nodded.

'You save my father's life,' Gog's son said hesitantly. 'He gave his for you.'

Dakkar shook his head. 'No,' he said. 'He gave it for you.'

Gog's son stood deep in thought then nodded solemnly. He extended a hand and Dakkar took it. For the first time, Dakkar saw Gog's son smile.

'Are you goin' to hold hands all day?' Mary called from the hatch of the *Liberty*. 'Only, I want to be gettin' home.'

Dakkar shook his head and climbed on board, giving a final wave to Gog's son and the giant warriors.

The *Liberty* felt warm inside and the engines pulsed. Georgia sat in the captain's seat and looked up. 'Ready, Dax?' she said.

'It's Dakkar,' Dakkar said.

'Dax.' Georgia grinned. 'Kinda fancy name, I reckon.'

Dakkar shook his head and Georgia pushed the drive lever to *Full Ahead*.

Dakkar sat on the lip of the hatch and waved to the giants as they shrank into the distance to become shrouded by trees along the riverbank. The jungle closed in around them once more.

'It's really quiet,' Dakkar said, scanning the bushes and undergrowth. 'It's as if when the tower blew up the wildlife fled from this whole area.'

'Maybe,' said Mary. 'Or perhaps when all them reptiles went back into the woods they ate everything in sight.'

'Who knows?' Dakkar murmured. Gweek glided down from the trees, a dragonfly caught in its toothy beak. It crunched at the insect, gulping it down. Dakkar grimaced. 'And what am I to do with you, little Gweek?'

'Aren't you going to keep it?' Mary asked.

'And how would I explain it to everyone on the surface world?' Dakkar said, running a finger along the top of the creature's scaly head.

'A bald parrot?' Mary smirked.

'It'll take us weeks to get to England,' Georgia called from the captain's seat. 'If you think I'm having that thing flying around and pooping on my head for all that time, you can think again.'

'I could make a cage,' Dakkar said, his heart sinking at the thought of leaving the little creature. Ugly as Gweek was, with its vicious rows of teeth, its leathery wings and scaly skin, he'd grown quite attached to it.

'If it's bonded with you,' Mary said, 'it'll follow you. What if it just flies and flies after you across the sea until it dies of exhaustion?'

'Kill it now then!' Georgia yelled.

'Georgia!' Dakkar snapped. 'That settles it – I'll make a cage.'

After much grumbling, Georgia beached the *Liberty* close to the ruins of the tower while Dakkar and Mary searched for suitable branches and sapling shoots to fashion a cage.

'Don't go too far into the forest,' Mary said, staring at the shadows.

Dakkar nodded, staring around at the silent ruins. The heap of rocks still smouldered; a few tiny lizards scampered about in the wreckage. Some distance away, a dark patch in the sand indicated where the bodies of the fallen giants had been. The Gacheela had taken every scrap and, so the giants believed, taken their souls into the skies.

Dumping an armful of green sticks into the lower cabin of the *Liberty*, Dakkar grinned at Georgia, who rolled her eyes.

'Couldn't we just make the cage and then leave Gweek here?' she said. 'It would escape eventually but we'd be long gone by then.'

Georgia popped her head out of the top of the *Liberty*. 'If that stupid bird thing of yours so much as farts in here, you'll wake up to find it roasted on a spit and served up for breakfast!'

Gweek landed on Dakkar's shoulder, gave a shriek and pecked his earlobe. 'Ow!' Dakkar said, rubbing his ear. 'You know I wouldn't let her do that! Just keep your head down, that's all.'

CHAPTER TWENTY-EIGHT
OUT ON THE OCEAN

They clambered into the *Liberty* and Georgia set her to *Full Ahead*.

Dakkar climbed down into the lower cabin of the craft, with Gweek sitting on his shoulder. He picked up the sticks and began to tie them together to form a cage. Mary came down and sat with him, tying some more sticks together. Soon they had two sides of a cube. The *Liberty* bounced and skipped across the waves.

'The sea tunnel is a good few days' sail from here,' Georgia called down from the upper cabin. 'The compass is hopeless so I'll have to try and remember the way.'

'Hopeless?' Dakkar repeated, putting down the cage and climbing up. The compass sat in a binnacle close to the *Liberty*'s wheel. It whirled around, never settling. 'Why is it doing that?'

Georgia shrugged. 'Maybe it's because we're deep beneath the earth's surface,' she suggested. 'North might be there.' She pointed upward. 'Or there.' she pointed at her feet.

'Let's hope you can remember the way then,' Dakkar murmured, staring through the portholes. He thought of the whale-like creature that had nearly dragged him below the waves. 'It could be worth travelling underwater for a while, so we can watch out for anything that might . . .'

'Want to eat us?' Georgia finished. She looked up at him, her face pale. 'Don't worry, I've been through this sea before. I know what you mean.'

'Did you use up all the Sea Arrows just getting here?' Dakkar said.

Georgia nodded and turned back to the wheel.

Mary had stopped tying up the cage when Dakkar returned to the lower cabin and was looking out of the large portholes set in the walls. Dakkar watched the scene outside as a shoal of huge fish, with toothed beaks like Gweek, weaved among each other.

'They remind me of dolphins,' Dakkar said, pressing a hand to the glass. 'Only their noses are longer.'

'That's what I found in the cliffs the other year,' Mary said. 'But it was a skeleton in the stone. How does something like that get to be turned to stone and stuck in the rocks up in Lyme?'

'Some say it was to do with the great flood that the Christian God sent,' Dakkar said slowly.

'You don't sound convinced,' Mary replied.

Dakkar shook his head. 'A natural philosopher once

told me that, thousands of years ago, a great catastrophe overtook the earth,' he said, watching the fish dart after prey. 'He wasn't sure what, but he said that the ground rose up and molten rock scorched the planet, turning everything into stone.'

'I'd believe anythin' after what I've seen these last few days,' Mary said, and smiled. She sat down and continued to tie up the sticks into a square lattice wall for the cage.

'Maybe these creatures are from another age,' Dakkar wondered aloud. 'Maybe that's why they aren't on the surface any more. Or maybe the ones on the surface met men like the count, who slaughtered them.'

They fell into silence, tying and fixing the sticks together. Before long, they had a rather rough but serviceable cage. Gweek protested when Dakkar tried to put it in, pecking at his fingers and screeching. Mary pushed a remaining stick across the middle of the cage as a perch and Gweek settled on to it, squeaking and grumbling as it preened itself.

The hours crawled by, inching into days. They had rewound the clock on board the *Liberty* but had no idea of the real time.

'Having the clock makes things worse in a way.' Dakkar sighed, staring at the hands that barely seemed to move. 'Time goes so slowly!'

Sometimes, Dakkar watched the strange parade of undersea life with Mary, something she never seemed to tire of. At other times, he would take over the helm of the *Liberty* and steer a straight course as directed by Georgia. They ate the black pineapple fruit when they were hungry.

'Save the dried meat in case we're down here longer than expected,' Georgia said.

Dakkar shuddered.

After almost a week – as far as they could tell – of travelling, Georgia began to spend more time at the helm, not trusting Dakkar.

'We must be close,' Georgia said, looking pale and worried. 'What if we miss a landmark when you're in control?'

'But you have to rest,' Dakkar insisted.

Finally, she agreed to take a break, but she had only the shortest of catnaps before taking over from Dakkar again.

'This is so frustrating!' Dakkar snapped.

'What?' Mary said, her face lit blue by the underwater scene outside.

'Cryptos may well be up there now,' Dakkar said, slapping his hand on the table. 'And here we are, miles away beneath the ground!'

'Grumblin' won't get us there any quicker,' Mary said, turning back to the porthole. 'Why don't you try and get Georgia to take a rest or somethin'?'

Dakkar climbed up to the top cabin and Georgia. Her brow was knotted with worry and she scanned the seabed.

'What's wrong?' Dakkar said, peering out at the sandy ocean floor. A thin veil of silt drifted across the ridged bed, giving the illusion that the ground moved.

'It all looks the same,' Georgia said, and bit her lip. 'I don't know where we're going.'

'We've kept a straight course, haven't we?' Dakkar said, laying a hand on her shoulder.

Georgia nodded.

'Then that's all we can trust in,' he said.

'But currents keep buffeting the *Liberty*. We could be miles away from the tunnel out of here,' Georgia whispered. 'Who knows how this underground sea flows?'

'Let me take the helm for a while,' Dakkar suggested. 'You can rest properly this time, and then take over again.'

Georgia nodded and let Dakkar slip into the seat as she stood up. Dakkar gave a brief grin. 'I promise not to sail into any rocks,' he said, glancing at her.

She gave a weary smile back, then frowned as if a dark thought had just flitted across her mind.

'Where did Mary come from, Dakkar?' Georgia said, her voice low and confidential.

'Come from?' Dakkar said, frowning. 'I met her in Lyme. I followed her down on one of Cryptos's Ascender Cages. She sneaks down to scavenge for stones and shells to sell. Why?'

'There's just something about her,' Georgia said, glancing down into the lower cabin.

'Oh, this is madness!' Dakkar said. 'You two have been arguing and bickering ever since you met. I don't know what you've got against her but we've got more important things to worry about.'

Georgia opened her mouth to speak but something flashed across the front of the *Liberty*. She leapt forward. 'What was that?' she said, craning her neck to see to the port side of the craft.

'Something big and fast,' Dakkar whispered. 'Get down below and load the Sea Arrows.'

CHAPTER TWENTY-NINE
DRAGGED TO DESTRUCTION

Dakkar strained his eyes staring into the depths of the water. Something had stirred up the silt on the seabed, making a fog of mud that shrouded everything. He slowed the *Liberty* down to a crawl, cursing under his breath. His heart thumped but a gnawing anxiety to be away also made him want to scream and ram the *Liberty* to *Full Ahead*.

'There!' Georgia called up from the lower cabin. 'Did you see it then?'

'Not from up here,' Dakkar said. 'What did it look like?'

'Hard to tell,' Georgia said, her voice strained. 'Big though.'

'What're we goin' to do?' Mary said, her voice feeble.

Gweek gave a similarly worried croak.

'It might be nothing,' Dakkar said, trying to keep his voice light. 'Maybe it's a plant-eater like those big lumps in the jungle and it's just trying to scare us off.'

The *Liberty* rocked and something thumped firmly against

her hull. A grating sound shivered through the planks that surrounded Dakkar. He gripped the wheel tightly, staring into the mud soup that whirled around them. Slowly, something red snaked its way across the porthole in front of him. A long, rubbery tentacle lined with row upon row of suckers. Dakkar recognised it right away.

'It's a giant squid,' he said, slamming the *Liberty* to *Full Ahead*. All his frustrations, all his worries evaporated. 'That noise is the squid's beak chewing the top of the *Liberty*. We've got to get it off.'

Whirling the friction-machine wheel, Dakkar counted each turn aloud. The tentacles swamped the craft now, blocking the view from the portholes and clinging to the glass.

'Twenty!' Dakkar shouted, and punched the red button.

The murky silt glowed blue and Dakkar felt the hairs on his arms prickle as the sea became charged with deadly electricity. The tentacles slid from the portholes and Dakkar flew back into his seat as the *Liberty* shot forward.

'Get those Sea Arrows ready!' Dakkar yelled, and he swung the *Liberty* into a ninety-degree turn so it faced the oncoming squid. *I only hope the ones I made actually work*, he thought.

'Ready,' Georgia called back to him.

Dakkar stared open-mouthed at the thing. It looked like a squid from the front but had at least ten tentacles, writhing and reaching for them. An enormous shell extended from behind its round eyes, a huge spike that disappeared off into the gloom of the sea.

'Fire!' Dakkar yelled. He heard the familiar *boing* of the arrow launcher and watched as the Sea Arrow hurtled towards the squid in a flurry of bubbles. 'That'll teach you a lesson.'

The arrow flew straight into the squid's gaping maw and exploded in a useless puff of black smoke.

'Oh,' said Dakkar. 'Try the other one!'

Georgia fired the second arrow. Dakkar bit his lip as the projectile hurtled from the *Liberty*. Once again the arrow failed to ignite.

'Ram it!' Mary cried, staring up from the lower hatch. 'I bet it's like a snail – it needs its shell to survive.'

Dakkar shrugged. He had nothing else, only one Sea Arrow that might not work. The squid hurtled towards them, ejecting water from its shell to propel it. The engines whined as Dakkar put the *Liberty* on a collision course with the creature.

Just as the squid threw open its tentacles to grab the *Liberty*, Dakkar blew some ballast and threw her up above the beast. He swerved round and sent the *Liberty* crashing against the squid's long shell. Dark brown sepia ink filled the water and Dakkar smiled at the rewarding cracking sound that echoed through the hull.

Dragging the *Liberty* upward, he caught a glimpse of shattered fragments of shell swirling in the sea. The creature began to sink as its shell filled with water, mingling with the ink and blood that boiled out in a thick dark cloud.

'You did it!' Mary shouted. 'We're safe!'

Dakkar's grin turned to a frown, though, as he dragged

at the controls. 'Something is pulling us backward,' he yelled, pushing at the craft's drive lever. The engine whined and gears clattered as the *Liberty* struggled to break away from whatever had caught her.

'The squid!' Georgia shouted.

Dakkar glanced up to see the squid carcass go flying past as if being sucked over a giant waterfall. Its round eye stared lifeless yet somehow accusingly as it flashed by.

'It's some kind of current,' Dakkar yelled. 'We're being dragged along by a powerful flow of water.'

He turned the *Liberty* round, hearing Mary and Georgia gasp as he did so. The sea seemed to have come alive in front of them, fashioning itself into a huge, gaping, sucking mouth. The dirt and silt that had been washed around further away rushed into the outline of a massive vortex.

'It's a maelstrom!' Dakkar yelled, slamming the *Liberty* into reverse.

'A what?' Mary said from below.

'A huge whirlpool,' Georgia shouted. 'Pulling everything into its heart and dragging it to destruction!'

'It's too strong!' Dakkar said, pushing and pulling on the drive lever. Both cabins filled with the smell of burning and hot metal as the engine tried to beat the irresistible force of the whirlpool.

'Shut down the engine,' Georgia shouted up. 'It'll catch fire. Our only hope is to try and ride it.'

'Catch hold of something then,' Dakkar said, shutting the engine off and gripping on to his seat.

Mud and seaweed swirled around them and then Dakkar's stomach lifted into his throat as the *Liberty* caught the first rotation of the pool. Dakkar's knuckles whitened as he gripped his seat. He heard a thump and a scream in the cabin below but couldn't look down as his head was being forced back against the chair.

Another crash and Gweek's screeches filled the cabin. The craft turned upside down, tipping Dakkar on to the upper hatch door and then dropping him through into the lower cabin as she righted again.

The lower cabin was a chaotic mess of overturned boxes, scattered fruit and barrels. Gweek screeched in protest, its cage on its side. Georgia tried to cling to the walls of the craft but staggered as the *Liberty* spun round and round. Mary lay on the floor, groaning, a large bruise blossoming on her forehead.

Dakkar retched as the *Liberty* tipped over again. A chair clipped his shoulder and black pineapple fruit bounced off the top of his head. Gweek's protests filled the cabin as the rolling grew faster. The whole of the cabin became a blur punctuated with painful impacts with fruit, barrels, furniture, even Georgia and Mary. There was nothing Dakkar could do to save himself.

Outside the porthole the water bubbled and pressed against the glass. Dakkar glimpsed droplets of water oozing in. Slapping a hand on the lip of the hatch to the upper cabin, Dakkar dragged himself up and somehow managed to throw himself back into the captain's seat.

Only his spinning head and the bile in his throat told

him that the *Liberty* was moving. Water gushed around them as if they were under a fountain. The force pushed him back into his seat, pressing on his chest and squeezing his breath out in short gasps. He reached out for the wheel with fingers like wet string.

We're going up, not down! Dakkar thought. *We're being sucked upward!*

The deluge of water cleared from the porthole, showing a round, black hole. They were being sucked straight into it. Dakkar coughed, trying to clear his burning lungs, and slapped his feeble hands on the ballast wheel, managing to blow the water from the hull cavity then, gradually, unconsciousness took him.

CHAPTER THIRTY

DUNCAN MACDONALD

A faint bumping sound brought Dakkar, groaning, to his senses. His head pounded and the inside of the upper cabin swum in front of him. The air in the *Liberty* tasted stale and his mouth felt dry.

'Am I dead?' he said, his voice hoarse.

Shaking himself and wincing, he looked out of the porthole. Raindrops speckled the glass, warping the view of a leaden sky and a grey, rolling sea. The chill air made him shiver. Wherever they were, it wasn't the warm, constantly dry underworld.

Something bumped against the *Liberty* again. Dakkar frowned, staring down at the lower cabin. Gweek squawked feebly, trapped by the ruins of its own cage. Mary's foot poked from under a pile of tarpaulins and chairs. Georgia was dragging herself to her feet, a task made more difficult by the pitching and tossing of the *Liberty* on the waves.

'Where are we?' she said, steadying herself on the wall of the cabin.

'I'm not sure,' Dakkar said, peering out of the porthole again. Then he gave a yell.

A tanned, bearded face filled his view. Dakkar glimpsed a bulbous nose and gappy, yellow teeth. The man gave a grin and tapped on the glass with a stubby finger.

'Looks like we have company,' Georgia said, helping Mary to stand up.

Dakkar pushed open the hatch to see the beaming face again. A fisherman wrapped in several coats, with grey, wiry hair over his shoulders, had tied his boat to the *Liberty* and was clinging to the deck.

'Are-ye-awright-laddie?' he said, his accent heavy and his voice muffled by his thick beard.

'Pardon?' Dakkar said, climbing out of the hatch. The cold sea breeze caught his breath and made his skin prickle.

'Ah said, are ye awright?' the fisherman said, slowing his voice down.

'Oh, yes.' Dakkar said. 'I'm fine. Erm, could you tell me where we are?'

'Ah, ye lost then.' The fisherman grinned. He extended a gnarled hand. 'Duncan MacDonald,' he said. 'I fish round these parts.'

'Yes,' Dakkar said, taking the man's hand. 'And what *are* these parts?'

Duncan scratched his beard. 'That's a funny-lookin' boat ye have there,' he said. 'Where are its sails?'

'We stowed them away,' Dakkar lied. He scanned the horizon, seeing a smudge of land in the distance. 'So, Mr MacDonald, where are we?'

'Well, that over there,' Duncan said, pointing at the land, 'that's Scotland. While over there,' he pointed in the other direction, 'that'd be Americay.' He wheezed with laughter at his own joke, doubling up and nearly slipping off the *Liberty*.

'Scotland?' Dakkar's heart leapt. 'Then we made it to the surface!' He slid back into the craft. 'We made it, Georgia! We made it back!'

Georgia grinned and then looked at the mess around them. 'We need time to clear up,' she began.

'No time,' Dakkar said, climbing down into the lower cabin. 'We can clear as we go. We have to get to Lyme.'

'If you don't mind me sayin', laddie,' Duncan called down. 'Ye look a wee bit of a mess. If you need a place to take stock, my cottage is just by the shore there. It'll be dark soon.'

He looked at Georgia, whose face sported a blue bruise and her lip a red cut. Mary stood blinking and coughing.

'Just one night then, thank you,' Dakkar said. 'We set sail at first light.'

Duncan's cottage proved to be almost as cramped as the *Liberty*: a tiny thatched croft on the edge of the shore, huddled in the shadow of two large mountains.

Duncan boiled a bubbling fish stew which made Dakkar's mouth water.

'Could I have a couple of the smaller fish please?' Dakkar asked him.

Duncan looked puzzled. 'Ye want them raw?'

'Erm, yes,' Dakkar said, his face reddening. 'I just like a bit of cold fish now and then.'

Eyeing Dakkar with raised eyebrows, Duncan handed over a couple of the sprats he was about to drop into the pot. Dakkar took them and hurried down to the *Liberty*, which lay semi-beached in the tide. He climbed aboard and down into the lower cabin, where Gweek sat in his repaired cage, hunched on his perch.

'Here you are,' Dakkar said, poking the fish through the bars.

Gweek snapped them up greedily and jerked them down his leathery throat.

'I think it would have been easier to explain the stupid lizard-bird thing than your taste for raw fish,' Georgia hissed on his return.

Duncan stirred the stew and chattered away in an accent so thick that Dakkar had trouble taking it all in. The fisherman marvelled over the *Liberty* and how she moved without sails. Dakkar muttered something about steam and cogs and pedals and Duncan nodded sagely, but was clearly baffled.

Duncan's cottage was so small and cramped that they sat at the low front door, sheltered by the overhanging roof and a small drystone wall, while they tried to explain where they'd come from.

'We were caught in a whirlpool,' Dakkar said, cradling

a bowl of stew in his hands. 'I passed out and when I awoke here we were.'

'An incredible tale.' Duncan shook his head. 'Where were ye before?'

'Iceland,' Georgia said.

'Norway,' Dakkar said.

'Somewhere round there,' Mary finished off.

'No wonder you're lost,' Duncan chuckled. 'You didn't even know where you were at the start.'

They slept in the byre that leaned against Duncan's ramshackle home. Stuffed with hay and straw, it proved warm and dry.

'Well, I'll bid ye a goodnight,' Duncan said, and closed the door on them.

'It's strange,' Georgia murmured drowsily. 'I never thought I'd be glad to see the dark again.'

'Can you see the dark?' Mary said, shuffling around in the hay.

'I know what you mean, though,' Dakkar said, his eyelids drooping. 'I'm still not sure what day or month it is or how long we were underground.'

'How *did* we get back up here?' Georgia said, yawning deeply.

'I think we were sucked up a waterspout,' Dakkar replied, rubbing his eyes. 'I saw them when the Gacheela tried to take me out to sea. They were huge columns of water. They must link to the sea on the surface. I don't know how they work though. Maybe something to do with pressure inside the earth or something . . .'

Georgia's snores were the only reply he got.

Dakkar grinned and grabbed a handful of straw. 'It's good to be back though,' he said in a whisper. He closed his eyes and fell into a dreamless sleep.

The warmth of the straw enveloped Dakkar and he relished the cold nipping at the tip of his nose while the rest of his body glowed. He stretched, wincing a little as his aching limbs reminded him of the battering he'd taken in the *Liberty*. A grey light filtered under the byre door but the thick stone walls sheltered them from the stiff wind that blew outside.

Dakkar smiled as he listened to the wind and the breathing of the others but a movement outside made him sit bolt upright. It wasn't a casual, leisurely footstep – somehow it sounded stealthy. As if someone were creeping up on the door.

Dakkar jumped to his feet as the door flew open, the square of sudden light blinding him momentarily.

'Don't move,' said a bulky figure filling the doorway.

Georgia leapt up but the room filled with bodies. Dakkar blinked as rough hands gripped his arms before his eyes could adjust.

'Get off me, you filthy bloody-back!' Georgia spat, tumbling past Dakkar as they spilled out of the byre.

Bloody-back? Dakkar thought. *That means redcoats. British soldiers!*

Eight marines in red coats and white breeches stood with their rifles ready, apart from the three who had hold of Dakkar, Georgia and Mary. Georgia pulled at the man's grip but he just laughed, a clay pipe clenched in his teeth.

Behind them, Duncan leapt about, wild eyed.

'I fetched ye,' he cried, throwing his arms in the air. 'Just like ye said I should. Anythin' suspicious, you said. Aye, well, these lot look suspicious enough to me.'

'You did well, Duncan,' said someone next to him. Dakkar couldn't see him properly as he was screened by the marines.

'Watch that one,' Duncan said, pointing at Dakkar. 'Eats raw fish, he does!'

Dakkar looked across to the *Liberty*. More red-coated soldiers stood hauling at the ropes that moored her to the beach. A rowing boat lay half in the water and beyond, out in the bay, a frigate waited, a Union flag fluttering at her stern.

'You sold us out!' Georgia yelled, lunging at Duncan, who cowered behind the line of armed marines.

'She's an American,' Duncan said. 'Aren't we at war with them?'

Dakkar frowned. The marines shuffled ranks a little, revealing the man Duncan was talking to. A tall thin man who had his back to them. He wore a black tricorne hat, a black jacket and his blond hair hung in a neat pigtail down his back.

'That other one, she sounds funny to me,' Duncan spat, pointing at Mary. 'She could be French!'

'French?' Mary shrieked. 'I'm from Dorset!'

The man turned round. A thin scar trickled down his

left cheek from the corner of his eye to his chin, making one half of his face sad and mournful.

'Commander Blizzard!' Dakkar gasped.

'So, Prince Dakkar of Bundelkhand,' Commander Blizzard said, raising an eyebrow, 'we meet again and, once again, under suspicious circumstances.'

CHAPTER THIRTY-ONE
PROJECT NEMO

Commander Blizzard stood in his cabin at the stern of the ship, arms behind his back. Dakkar gazed out of the square windows that lined the rear of the frigate and watched the islands slowly vanish behind him. Georgia sat in a chair glowering at Blizzard while Mary clasped her hands, her face as pale as the commander's.

'I seem to recall a similar situation only last year,' Blizzard mused, pacing up and down his cabin. 'Me asking questions and you being exceptionally reticent with the answers, Dakkar.'

'With all due respect, commander,' Dakkar said, arms folded, 'I'm not sure you'd believe me if I told you.'

'I think you'd be surprised at how much faith I have in you, Dakkar,' Blizzard said, his voice mild. 'We came up here investigating reports of strange sea beasts. We all know what that means. And what do we find? You three – two of you wearing Cryptos uniforms – with what looks like a submersible and the strangest bird I've ever set eyes on.'

Gweek sat on his perch in the cage. The marines had brought it out of the *Liberty* at the commander's orders.

'He's a bald parrot,' Mary blurted out.

Blizzard smirked and threw his hands in the air. 'If you can't offer me a suitable explanation then I'll have to assume that you're spies.'

'I thought you'd drowned,' Dakkar said. Blizzard had commanded the HMS *Palaemon*, a frigate that Georgia had rammed with the *Liberty*, sending her to the bottom of the sea last year.

'No, we had time to reach the boats and only lost one man,' Blizzard said. He narrowed his eyes at Georgia. 'We never knew what it was that sunk the *Palaemon*, although I'm beginning to have my suspicions.'

Georgia glanced out of the window, avoiding Blizzard's searching gaze.

Dakkar bit his lip. Every minute they wasted here meant more time for Stefan to organise his troops and put his plan into action. Blizzard had the *Liberty* winched up to the side of the ship. Escape was almost impossible.

'All right,' Dakkar said. 'I'll tell you, but then you've got to help us.'

'Dakkar, no!' Georgia said, leaping up from her seat.

'Are we going to stop the count alone?' Dakkar said, looking Georgia straight in the eye. 'We need help.'

'If I can help, I will,' Blizzard said. 'I haven't forgotten how you saved my life, Dakkar. You fought bravely at my side last time we met. That counts for a lot.'

Dakkar pulled up a chair and began to tell Blizzard everything from the beginning. He omitted any mention of Cutter's Cove, saying that he'd managed to get Oginski to Lyme on his own. By the time he'd finished his tale, Blizzard sat stroking his chin.

'I must confess, Dakkar,' he said, 'you're a superb story-teller, and were it not for the strange bird sitting on my table I would have difficulty believing you. So old Boney an impostor, eh?'

'But we must hurry to Brussels,' Dakkar said, running his fingers through his hair. 'Count Cryptos will be assembling his forces near there.'

'By all accounts, he's had a few weeks to get organised,' Blizzard said, frowning. 'He will have had plenty of time.'

'Then we can't waste any more,' Dakkar said.

Blizzard pursed his lips. 'You're right, of course. Come, we'll set a course immediately.'

Georgia folded her arms. 'I suppose you think that's funny,' she said.

'I don't know what you mean?' Blizzard stared at her, his eyebrows raised.

'You've no more intention of taking us to the Low Countries than I have of sprouting wings and flying to Philadelphia!' Georgia snorted.

'Young lady,' Blizzard said, wincing a little at her tone, 'I'm not at all sure of *your* intentions. I suspect they were somewhat hostile when last you came near one of my

ships. If you do intend to sprout wings, could you fore-
warn me? I've had enough surprises for one day. In the
meantime, come with me and I will explain.'

Blizzard led them out of his quarters and on to the main
deck. The cold air struck Dakkar and he shivered. Men
scurried about, securing ropes and shouting incompre-
hensible orders to each other. Dakkar remembered his
last jaunt with Blizzard, spending half the time as a prisoner and the other half scrubbing decks. But he'd ended
up saving Blizzard's life and he suspected that he had a
true ally in the commander.

'Welcome aboard the HMS *Slaughter*,' Blizzard said,
making a theatrical gesture.

'Lovely name,' Georgia muttered, still blushing from
Blizzard's stinging rebuff.

'These men are hand-picked,' Blizzard continued.
'Signed up for life, sworn to secrecy and totally loyal to
me. It's Britain's answer to Cryptos. Our orders come
from the highest authority. We are to track down any
activity by Cryptos and we answer to nobody but the
King himself. If we are caught, nobody will help us. If we
succeed, no honours will be given. As far as the navy is
concerned, we don't exist. Secrecy is our strength. This
is Project Nemo.'

'One ship?' Dakkar said, looking dubiously at Blizzard.

'If it were just one ship, I would share your scepti-
cism,' Blizzard said, patting the mainmast as if it were
a horse. 'But Project Nemo is well armed and has
many facets.'

'Why are you telling us this if it's all so secret?' Georgia said, narrowing her eyes.

'Because I hope it shows that I'm serious when I say we are heading for Brussels now,' Blizzard said. 'And I hope that, one day, you'll join us.'

'Well, we're kinda stuck on your ship,' Georgia said. 'And I don't suppose you'll let us hop into the Liberty and sail away.'

Blizzard laughed. 'Miss Fulton,' he said, 'if you wish to leave on your craft, please feel free to do so. Such is my faith that our causes are very closely entwined.'

'You'd just let us go?' Dakkar said, astounded.

'We are sailing at full tilt for Ostend, Dakkar,' Blizzard said, clenching his fist. 'We are fighting a common enemy. I'd be lying if I said I didn't want to find out more about your undersea craft but there are more pressing matters. One day you may share your secrets for the good of all, but for now we have Cryptos to defeat.'

Dakkar bit his lip, looking from Georgia to Blizzard. 'Very well,' he said.

'Don't trust him,' Georgia snapped. 'He just wants to get his hands on the Liberty.'

'If I wanted to get the Liberty, I could have had you shot back at that hovel on the island.' Blizzard's pale cheeks actually reddened. 'I could have had you thrown overboard an hour ago.' He took a breath and turned to Dakkar. 'I promise that none of my men will go near your precious submersible.'

'It's not his – it's mine,' Georgia said.

'Georgia, that's enough,' Dakkar said, losing patience himself. 'We must focus on the job at hand. Cryptos will be rallying his forces.'

'Our sources tell us that Napoleon is building his army,' Blizzard said, staring out to sea. 'They will be ready to strike within days.'

The journey to the Low Countries was a flurry of activity. Dakkar gave Blizzard as much detail as he could about how the Cryptos Riders were armed, their tactics, the size of the lizards they rode.

Blizzard shook his head. 'I don't think I'll actually believe you until I see one of these creatures myself,' he said.

'The fear they strike into the hearts of their opponents is half their danger,' Dakkar said, shivering a little at the memory of them.

Georgia remained aloof, keeping close to the *Liberty*, which now sat on the main deck draped in tarpaulins. All around her, marines sharpened bayonets, checked powder stores or practised loading drill.

'The faster they load, the more enemies we can bag before we resort to close combat,' Blizzard remarked.

Mary kept to Blizzard's quarters, avoiding the preparations for battle. 'I'm not a fighter,' she said. 'And if you could drop me off at Lyme before you go chargin' off, I'd be most grateful.'

Dakkar pursed his lips. He would relish the chance to go and check on Oginski. The thought that he might be dead gnawed at him all the more, the closer they got to their destination. Rounding Land's End, Dakkar could see the familiar rocky cliffs. *I'm so close to the castle*, he thought. *I wish I could be there now, with Oginski helping me dismantle a steam engine or a clock – or anything, in fact.*

'If only we could,' Blizzard said to Mary. 'But every minute counts.'

'You can look after Gweek,' Dakkar said, feeling stupid the moment the words left his lips.

'Yeah,' Georgia muttered. 'You kind of suit each other.'

'That's enough,' Dakkar said, staring intently at Georgia. *What has she got against Mary?*

Much of the time was taken up with poring over maps of France and the Netherlands, trying to figure out where Cryptos may be hiding.

'If we knew how many men and animals he had, that would give us a chance,' Blizzard said, looking hopefully at Dakkar for what seemed like the tenth time.

'I know,' Dakkar sighed. 'Many of the lizard riders were embarking when I set off the explosives but how many got to the surface . . .?' He shrugged.

'I suggest we search the area here.' Blizzard stabbed the map with his finger. 'There are a number of large farm buildings that may house this infernal cavalry.'

'It may be that a lot of livestock has been taken from around his camp,' Dakkar said, thinking aloud. 'The lizards would take a lot of feeding.'

'You're right,' Blizzard said, nodding his approval. 'Our scouts will question locals wherever possible.'

The port grew closer and Dakkar looked longingly out to sea, where England lay. *To think I'd ever miss the place*, he thought. *I used to hate it.*

The coast of Belgium grew ever nearer and ships thronged the English Channel.

'They bring supplies, men, weapons,' Blizzard said, his scarred face looking grim. 'All the things needed to wage war.'

The arrival of the HMS *Slaughter* went largely unnoticed amid the bustle of Ostend port. The stone quay was lined with ships of all sizes. It bristled with masts and yardarms and teemed with soldiers, marines, sailors and dockers. Gangs of white-whiskered dock workers hurled sacks of grain from the sides of ships while carts rattled up and down the cobbled walkways. The smell of tobacco and meat cooking mingled with tar and the sea. Dakkar leaned over the side of the ship and listened to the strange languages drifting up from the crowd of men. He could pick out bits of French and some German too. The dock workers spoke a language with which he was unfamiliar.

Blizzard requisitioned some carts and his men began to load them up. Dakkar watched as more and more supplies came out of the hold. Within a few hours, Blizzard stood at the head of a column of a hundred marines and several carts carrying powder, food and trailing cannon.

'Right,' Blizzard said, turning to Dakkar and Georgia. 'Let's go and hunt some lizards!'

CHAPTER THIRTY-TWO
TERROR IN THE DARK

A day's march brought them deep into the countryside. Dakkar couldn't see much difference between this land and England. True, in Cornwall, the lanes lay deep between high hedges and it was a much more rugged landscape. Here, the land undulated and fields formed a patchwork across the rolling hills. The sky hung above them like a sodden grey rag, threatening to wring its moisture out over their heads at any moment.

'When do we stop?' Georgia muttered to Dakkar.

'I did suggest that you stay at the ship with Miss Anning and Dakkar's strange bird,' Blizzard said, overhearing her. There had been something of a scene at the quayside when Blizzard had suggested that Georgia stayed behind. Mary had cheerfully agreed, hurrying to the commander's quarters, but Georgia had stood with her hands on her hips.

'In a sow's eye I will!' she'd declared, squaring up to the commander.

'I'd trust Georgia with my life in combat, sir,' Dakkar had cut in, trying to diffuse the situation.

Blizzard had pursed his lips and walked away without comment but he made no objection when Georgia walked alongside him and Dakkar.

Now they stood, footsore and weary, in a cold field.

'Here's as good as anywhere to set up camp,' Blizzard said, looking at the map. 'We'll wait for the carts and supplies to catch up.'

By dark, they were huddled around a campfire, supping on a thick stew. It tasted good to Dakkar, warming him after the day's long march. Sentries kept watch just beyond the glow of the fire. The summer sky hadn't truly darkened but the thick cloud cast a gloom of its own.

'We travel due south tomorrow,' Blizzard said, stirring his spoon in the bowl of stew. 'That will bring us into the region where Bonaparte told you Cryptos may be based. If nothing else we'll be well placed to stop them attacking Wellington's forces from behind.'

'Wellington?' Dakkar frowned. 'I had forgotten he led the Alliance's forces.'

'You don't sound too enamoured, Prince Dakkar,' Blizzard said, a mischievous grin on his face.

'He fought my uncle, the Sultan Tipu, at Seringapatam many years ago,' Dakkar said. He felt an ember of anger flare in his stomach.

'Ah,' Blizzard said.

'What's that meant to mean?' Georgia said, her voice thick with stew. 'Seringapa . . . what?'

'The Duke of Wellington defeated the Sultan,' Blizzard explained. 'In India, some years ago. Before you were born.'

'He killed him,' Dakkar murmured. 'It was a dark day for my family.'

'All's fair in love and war,' Blizzard said, staring at Dakkar. 'So they say.'

Dakkar stalked off to his tent. He sat inside, unable to sleep. *Why am I even here?* he thought. *What do I care if these dogs eat each other?* Then he thought of Gog straining to hold up the ceiling, buying vital seconds with his life. He thought of Oginski lying on his deathbed and Napoleon's cold, stone tomb. He thought of the promise he had made to stop the count. He lay down and stared out of the tent into the night.

Sleep must have come to Dakkar at some point because he awoke to the sound of screaming and the bitter chill that seems to settle just before dawn. He leapt to his feet and staggered out of the tent. Rain pelted down on the camp, rattling on the canvas covers. The whole area swarmed with half-dressed marines. Men shouted and musket fire split the air.

Dakkar rubbed his eyes. Two sentries lay dead on the grass just beyond the tents. A reptile rider, in resplendent blue French uniform, charged straight at him through the middle of the camp. The Rohaga's mount strode on two huge back legs, churning up the sodden ground. Its small front ones hung uselessly in front of it. Armour shielded its face and breast but its belly was exposed. It thundered towards him.

A few marines fell back, wide eyed at the sight of the ferocious beast. Blizzard stepped out from the line of tents and brandished his sword.

'Come on, lads!' he bellowed. 'You've seen worse than this. Form ranks and prepare to fire!'

Enough of the soldiers, although ragged from sleep, formed a line and loaded their rifles. Dakkar noticed a few fumbling at the musket barrels and dropping powder. He snatched up his own empty rifle, holding it like a club, and stood crouched, ready to defend himself. His heart pounded as he shook the rainwater from his eyes. The rider's polished breastplate shone behind the snarling head full of teeth that hurtled towards him.

As it came closer, Dakkar could smell the reptile's rank breath, see its round yellow eye. He swung his rifle butt at the thing's nose but the air sounded with a single explosion as ten guns went off in unison. Musket balls peppered the creature, bringing it to the ground. It peddled its powerful rear legs, trying to attack the pain that seared its body. The rider lay pinned beneath it, swearing in French at Dakkar.

But Blizzard's marines had already reloaded and another volley blasted into the writhing mass. Both rider and reptile lay still.

The sound of the gunfire drifted off into the leaden clouds. Dakkar could hear the men's panting breath. Someone vomited; another man swore under his breath.

Blizzard strolled over to the fallen reptile and rested a foot on it. He turned to his marines and nodded.

'Well done, men,' he bellowed. 'You let your training take control and showed steely nerve. You can see what we're up against but you now know that this creature bleeds too. We'll meet more of them, that's a certainty. Are we afraid?'

'No!' the men replied in a gruff, bass chorus.

'Yes,' muttered Dakkar to Georgia.

'God save the King!' Blizzard yelled, and his marines howled back, punching their fists in the air.

Blizzard encouraged the men to come forward and look at the reptile. The marines grinned, kicking at the carcass, jabbing its leathery skin with their bayonets and discussing where it was most vulnerable.

Later, with the camp packed, they marched on, leaving the reptile and its rider blazing on a pyre of logs.

'We don't want to leave any evidence,' Blizzard had said as his men poured oil over the fire to encourage it to burn. 'Such a monster may cause a panic.'

'That had to be a scout of some description,' Dakkar said. 'We were lucky to catch it broadside and on its own. Things might be different with a whole squadron bearing down on us. From the front, their armour protects them.'

'We'll be ready,' Blizzard said. 'My men have fought fearsome beasts before. Some of them faced the giant squid that nearly killed me last year.'

'We have to find Cryptos,' Georgia said. 'Before the battle starts.'

'I fear the battle has already begun,' Blizzard said, peering over at the rising smoke on the horizon.

Dakkar listened as the low growl of cannon echoed across the fields towards them and was answered by the snap of musket fire.

CHAPTER THIRTY-THREE
THE BATTLE

They marched on, skirting the sounds of battle. Dakkar shivered at the crack and pop of musket fire and the deeper roar of cannon. The clatter of thousands of men fighting drifted on the wind. He'd been in some dangerous situations before and seen conflict but never a full-scale battle.

'We'll keep to the west of the fighting,' Blizzard said as they marched through a small wood. 'If Cryptos planned to outflank the Alliance, it would be around here somewhere.'

'Look!' Georgia cried, pointing.

As they broke from the cover of the trees, the land opened out. Dakkar peered at a thin line of men in green uniforms with yellow flashes at their cuffs and collars. He was surprised at how close they were. A field of flattened wheat separated Blizzard's men and the other soldiers.

'Dutch infantry, I'd guess,' Blizzard said, sniffing. 'They're forming a line.'

'I think we've found our quarry,' Dakkar said, nodding to his right.

A line of reptile riders approached the line of Dutch soldiers at a stalking pace. They looked strange and unreal from this distance. The riders' breastplates shone in the watery sun and the reptiles leaned forward, poking their heads towards the Dutch infantry. Dakkar counted around fifty Rohaga.

'We've caught them unawares and on the side!' Blizzard said, punching his fist into his palm. 'Lady Luck smiles on us today.'

'Let's hope she keeps smiling,' Georgia said, craning her neck at the distant riders.

'Look! In the centre of the pack!' Dakkar said, pointing. 'It's him – the count.'

One reptile stood out as larger than all the others. On top of it rode the bulky figure of the count, his black hair streaming out behind him. A rider next to him held a flag that bore the serpent-entwined C for Cryptos over the French tricolour.

'Right, men, pass it back,' Blizzard said to the foremost of his marines. 'I want two lines for flanking volley fire on that field boundary there and our field guns set up behind them. Quick now! And keep it silent. Surprise is our best ally. After that, it's a hard-fought battle. Good luck!'

The order went back and the marines ran across the fields, keeping low. Dakkar watched others unhitch the cannon and begin dragging them through the heavy soil of the field that had been saturated with rain all night. They all ran forward. Dakkar watched the scene unfold before him as the riders increased their pace.

'Some are running away!' Georgia gasped, watching as a few soldiers broke from the Dutch line.

'Can you blame them?' Dakkar said, his breath short. 'They've just seen the reptiles for the first time.'

The reptile riders had covered half the field now and Dakkar could see the muscles rippling on their flanks and thighs as they sprinted towards the Dutch line. A few Dutch guns went off early, men panicking at the sight of the oncoming creatures.

Blizzard's men had set up their five cannon and had them loaded and ready. Either side of them, the marines stood in lines, their guns held high. Dakkar knew what would happen – Blizzard had explained their strategy. The first line fired their rifles and then knelt down to reload while the rear line fired. If there was time, they would give another volley of fire and so on.

'Fire!' Blizzard yelled.

All five cannon roared at once, leaping back on their wheels with the recoil. As the smoke cleared from around them, Dakkar watched the cannonballs carve a bloody path through the middle of the reptile cavalry. The creatures stumbled and careered into each other, crushing their riders or throwing them under the trampling feet of the others. One evaporated in a red mist as the cannonball went straight through it.

'That had to be ten down!' Dakkar yelled, punching the air.

Another round tore into the rear of the pack. Once more the cannonballs went skittering across the field, churning up the earth and sending the reptiles screaming into each other. More riders fell, their mounts turning on other loose and wounded reptiles.

But Dakkar watched in horror as the remaining reptile cavalry fell upon the Dutch ranks. Men screamed, firing their muskets randomly before falling to tooth and claw. The riders swung heavy sabres which lopped limbs and heads while the soldiers tried to escape. A lone officer dropped his sword and stumbled across the field, crying for help as a rider closed in on him.

A marine sergeant looked back at Blizzard, who gave a nod.

The marine raised his rifle, took aim and shot the reptile in the head just as it was about to lay its claws into the officer's back.

'Look to, men,' Blizzard shouted.

'We've gained their attention!' Dakkar frowned, wondering what Blizzard could mean, until he looked back at the field.

Not wasting time to tear at the fallen soldiers, the reptiles had turned and were reforming, ready to charge at the marines.

'Canister!' Blizzard cried, and the cannon crew dragged some strange cylinders and rammed them into the cannon.

Dakkar looked puzzled.

'Chains, lead shot, nails, anything,' Georgia muttered to him. 'It's all in those cylinders, and when they come out of the cannon, red hot . . .'

Dakkar shuddered. 'Against ordinary men, it seems a cowardly way to fight.'

'Against these beasties, it might just even the odds,' Blizzard cut in. 'You'd best arm yourselves.' He turned to his men and commanded them to stand ready.

Dakkar marvelled at Blizzard's presence. He would fight alongside his men and die with them if needs be. For a moment, Dakkar thought of Gog and of the real Napoleon, leaping in to save him. They were real leaders – not like the count, who ruled by fear.

'Come on!' Georgia yelled, grabbing him and dragging him over to the carts that stood behind the ranks.

They climbed up on to the nearest cart, grabbing two rifles from the supplies and hastily loading them. Glancing up, Dakkar saw the reptile riders getting nearer and nearer. There had to be thirty left. He could see the flag and the count, pointing his sabre at the lines of red-coated marines before him.

'What's this?' Georgia said, pulling the lid off a wooden crate to reveal what looked like a pile of iron cricket balls with fuses.

'Hand grenades.' Dakkar grinned, pulling out a tinder-box from his pocket. 'Light that lantern there but keep it away from the explosives!'

'I know, I know,' Georgia said, striking the tinderbox and kindling a flame.

Blizzard ran over. 'Stay on the carts,' he said. 'It'll keep you safe and give you height when they break through the lines. Do as much damage as you can!'

'Aye, sir,' Georgia said, giving a mock salute.

Blizzard raised an eyebrow and turned back to his soldiers.

The reptiles were close now, kicking up great clods of earth as they skittered across the field, their riders giving a bloodthirsty roar.

'Ready, lads. Aim for the reptiles,' Blizzard said, readying his own rifle. 'We can deal with the scum on top when they're pinned under their dead mounts!'

The marines' first volley fired and Dakkar watched, dismayed, as the bullets pinged off the armour. Only one or two caught a vulnerable spot, sending the reptiles crunching into the dirt and throwing their riders headlong towards the line.

The cannon fired next, drowning the whole company in a fog of gun smoke. Five canisters of red-hot metal spat through the advancing ranks. Dakkar heard screams and men's cries, growls of agonised rage. But Blizzard didn't flinch.

'Fire!' he cried, and the second rank of marines let their rifles roar into the mass.

The smoke had cleared somewhat and through the thin veil of mist Dakkar saw reptiles clambering over a wall of dead. Riders lay trapped under their mounts and more of the creatures piled on top of them. But the line behind leapt over their fallen comrades. The cannon crew reloaded, but the reptiles crashed through them before they could fire, overturning the guns, slashing at men, biting and ripping.

With a shiver Dakkar realised they were right in the path of the oncoming horde.

Georgia grinned, shouldering her rifle. 'Better get shootin', Dakkar.'

The mass of reptiles swarmed around the carts, rocking them. Dakkar fired his first rifle, catching a rider in the shoulder and sending him spinning down from his mount.

Snatching up a grenade, he lit the fuse from the lantern and waited a second before hurling it blindly into the press of scaly bodies. A muffled thump told him that it had exploded. A reptile screamed, sank to its knees and was quickly engulfed by its trampling companions.

The cavalry charge swept past them so quickly that Dakkar almost lit another grenade before he realised they had vanished up the field. Two or three dead reptiles lay scattered around the cart but the cavalry were wheeling round. He could see them reining in their two-legged mounts, readying them for another charge. The cannon lay useless, most of the crew dead on the ground. A few tried to right one of the guns, heaving at its wheels.

Blizzard barked an order and the marines sprinted forward, forming a new line to face the next charge. The Rohaga thundered back across the field, the count's face a mask of cruelty, grinning as he pointed his sabre.

'Ready,' Blizzard said. 'Give 'em hell!'

The marine line exploded again, sending more reptiles to the ground, but this time the cavalry pulled their mounts up and slashed with their sabres.

Dakkar snatched up his rifle and fired at a rider who slashed at a marine. The bullet took him in the thigh, making him drop his sword and grip his leg. But before the marine could react, the rider's mount snapped down, sinking razor teeth into the marine's shoulder.

Human yells and screams mingled with reptilian roars and hisses. Grabbing a grenade, Dakkar lit and hurled it under a passing rider. It exploded, opening up the creature's belly and sending the rider crunching to the ground.

Georgia took another rider down with her second rifle.

'Better load up again,' she yelled. 'Keep throwing those grenades.'

Dakkar went to hurl another but the battle had become compacted around the carts and the explosion would kill as many marines as Rohaga.

Blizzard stood on the carcass of a dead beast, desperately parrying the sabre hacks of its rider. Georgia had loaded the first rifle and passed it to Dakkar, who took aim and fired at the man attacking Blizzard.

The bullet careened off the man's silver helmet, dazing him. Blizzard knocked the sword from his hand and stabbed, sending the rider to the ground. He turned and nodded to Dakkar, but a loose beast clamped its jaws on to Blizzard's arm, yanking him off his feet.

'No!' Dakkar yelled, as Blizzard disappeared into the melee.

The reptile bounded off across the field. Blizzard clung to its head, his legs wrapped round its neck, his arm still locked in its mouth. He stabbed and stabbed at its eye and throat with a dagger but couldn't get free.

'Dakkar, look out!' Georgia screamed.

He turned to see a mounted rider, level with the cart, and his keen blade humming down towards him.

CHAPTER THIRTY-FOUR
A LOSING BATTLE

Dakkar ducked and a sword whistled over his head. The rider hacked at him again, slicing his sabre sideways at Dakkar's legs. Dakkar leapt up but stumbled forward and fell off the cart and on to the rider.

He brought his elbow up, jabbing the rider desperately in the throat. The man gave a gargling cough and Dakkar dragged his helmet over his eyes before shoving him over the back of his mount.

The beast snapped and growled, trying to shake Dakkar from the saddle. Dakkar gripped the reins tightly, rolling with the writhing of the reptile.

'Grenade!' he shouted to Georgia.

She lit a grenade and threw it to him. Catching it, he leaned forward so the reptile could see his head. It swung round, opening its wide jaws and giving Dakkar a blast of foul breath.

Dakkar rammed the grenade down its throat and leapt

for the cart as the creature erupted in an explosion of red that splattered all around.

Landing awkwardly on the cart, Dakkar grabbed at another rifle. The fight was going badly for the marines even though they had outnumbered the riders two to one. Many had managed to unseat their opponents but that left one marine dealing with the rider and the other with a vicious killing machine. Bodies of marines and Rohaga lay strewn around the carts.

The last few marines huddled around the carts, stabbing with bayonet and sword. Stefan blew a whistle and the remaining riders withdrew, reforming a line some distance away.

Dakkar shuddered. They were getting ready for a final charge.

All he could hear was the panting of the marines and the distant rumble of battle. He counted the reptiles quickly. *Fifteen*, he thought, glancing down with a sinking heart, *and only eight men.*

Stefan blew his whistle again and the reptiles began their walk towards the remaining men.

Dirt and blood streaked the marines' faces but Dakkar could see the fire in their eyes.

'Don't worry, lad,' one man said, looking up at him. 'There were fifty of 'em to start with. We can finish them.'

'I have a better idea,' Dakkar said, looking down at the boxes of grenades and kegs of powder. 'I want you to run away.'

'Don't be daft,' said another marine. 'With all due respect, sir.'

Dakkar grinned. 'Well, I'm going to blow this cart up when the reptiles come past here, so either you can stay or you can run and bring them here a bit quicker.'

'Apologies for calling you daft, sir,' the marine said. He turned to the other seven. 'Come on, boys. It's time for a run.'

'Dakkar! What if it doesn't work and you're caught out in the open?' Georgia said, gripping his arm.

'If you've got a better idea, I'm happy to hear it,' he replied.

She shook her head.

'Good,' he said. 'Then get running. I'll catch you up!'

Georgia gave one backward glance and then jumped off the cart.

The Rohaga were nearer now, their pace increasing. Dakkar gave a final salute to the marines and Georgia, and then they began to run across the field.

The Rohaga riders gave a shout and lifted their swords.

'As I suspected, they couldn't resist a chase.' Dakkar smiled as the riders kicked their reptiles on to a sprint.

Stefan hung back with his flag bearer, yelling at them and blowing his whistle. He'd realised the danger, but his cavalry were eager for blood and charged straight at the cart to get to the remaining marines.

They were close now. Dakkar could hear the men hollering and whooping, see their grins as they urged their mounts on. Dakkar lit his grenade and jumped down off the cart. He turned and tossed the grenade back up on to the pile of boxes and ran.

The explosion threw Dakkar across the field, the roar deafening him. It felt as if someone had punched him in the back. He rolled and tumbled like a leaf blown in a gale, his ears ringing. He lay still, blinking in disbelief at the power of the blast.

The ruined cart lay smouldering; an axel leaning on one wheel was all that remained. Smoking fragments and embers littered the ground all around Dakkar. One lone reptile leapt and hopped, trying to stand on a broken leg. The rest lay among the dead on the field.

Dakkar staggered to his feet, the marines cheering behind him, but his grin froze as the smoke cleared to reveal the count and his flag bearer racing towards him.

Dakkar glanced around for anywhere to shelter. The overturned cannon lying a few yards away were the only kind of cover. Snatching up a fallen sabre, he sprinted to them. Georgia and the remainder of the marines hurried back towards him. Dakkar realised they had had the chance to reload but Stefan would be on top of him before they could get within decent firing range.

Stefan's eyes widened as he saw Dakkar. He urged the reptile on towards Dakkar, shouting at the flag bearer, who lowered the flagstaff's pointed end, turning it into a deadly lance, then charged at the marines and Georgia.

'I should've killed you when I had the chance!' Stefan shouted as he reached Dakkar.

'You tried, remember?' Dakkar said, scurrying round

the cannon as Stefan's reptile snapped at him over the wheel. 'You pushed me off the tower.'

The beast lunged at him again, planting its claws on the wheels of the cannon. Dakkar jabbed with the heavy cavalry sabre. It felt unbalanced and awkward in his hands but it made the reptile recoil.

Stefan wheeled the creature round so that he could slash down at Dakkar. The gun that lay on its side between them made it difficult for Stefan to hack accurately and Dakkar easily parried the blows. Metal rang on metal as the force numbed his arm.

Stefan slashed again and again, forcing Dakkar to skirt round the cannon and even duck under it.

Somewhere across the field the marines let off a volley at the flag bearer. Dakkar glanced over, seeing the man fall from his mount, but the reptile thundered on towards the marines who stood, bayonets ready, braced for the attack. Georgia was reloading quickly behind them.

'Just keep still,' Stefan snapped, clanging his sword off the cannon barrel and sending sparks flying. 'I promise you a swift end!'

Dakkar scrambled under the cannon and jabbed the sword into the reptile's leg. The beast hissed and leapt back, almost unseating Stefan. But Dakkar was exposed now and Stefan recovered enough to swipe his blade across, almost taking the top off Dakkar's head.

Quickly jumping back round the carriage, Dakkar glanced over to Georgia. The other reptile had taken one of the marines in its jaws and the others stabbed at it with their bayonets. He saw its tail lash round and send another soldier stumbling backward.

'Your reptile cavalry is destroyed,' Dakkar said, panting as he skipped round the carriage, trying to avoid Stefan. 'Give up!'

'You may have stopped my cavalry, but when the French forces win the main battle I will take control,' Stefan snarled. 'First, I'll enjoy feeding you to my little pet here.'

'You'll have to catch me,' Dakkar said breathlessly.

'I can wait.' Stefan grinned. 'You are tiring already.'

He slashed down with his sword again, catching Dakkar's blade and then sweeping it aside. Dakkar watched in despair as the sabre flew from his numbed grip and landed among the glowing fragments of the exploded cart.

The reptile gave a low, guttural growl and, with a click of encouragement from its master, set one foot on the upturned wheel of the cannon. The big gun rocked and tipped upright as the reptile stood on it.

'Soon you will join my sanctimonious brother,' Stefan sneered. 'I've made sure he's finished, and now I'll finish you!'

But Dakkar was looking at the reptile's foot. It rested on the cannon's wheel and the muzzle was pressed hard against the creature's chest.

'Not if I can help it,' Dakkar said, stooping down and snatching up a red-hot ember from the cart. 'The cannon crew had just managed to reload when you hit them. They were about to fire. I'll finish the job, shall I?'

Stefan's eyes widened and he snagged at the reins of the reptile but Dakkar, ignoring the searing pain from the ember, pressed it against the vent at the back of the barrel.

'Noooo!' the count roared, but the deafening boom of the cannon cut short his cry as he vanished in a cloud of smoke and blood, liquidised by the hail of hot metal that spewed from the muzzle of the cannon. Dakkar saw the reptile's head fly up out of the cloud, closely followed by a human arm.

At the same time, the cannon kicked back, crunching into Dakkar and sending him breathless and dazed to the ground.

The world tilted on its side as Dakkar lay there, staring across the field. He felt detached and hazy as he watched the one remaining reptile closing in on Georgia and the last few marines, who jabbed with their rifles and bayonets.

And then he heard a chilling scream as if all the demons of Hell had been focused into one voice and unleashed across the battlefield.

CHAPTER THIRTY-FIVE

AN END TO EVERYTHING

Sitting up on the ground, Dakkar watched, his mouth hanging wide open as a second reptile stormed across the field. Blizzard sat on its back, his arm flapping like a shredded piece of red cloth, his good hand gripping the reins tightly.

Gore streamed from the reptile's eyes down its face and it was clear that it was blind. Blizzard pointed it straight at the monster harrying his marines and as it collided with the other reptile, he leapt off, rolling on the ground to safety. The blind reptile, in a fury of pain and confusion, tore into the neck of this new enemy. Together they bit and scratched, ripping huge chunks of flesh from each other until, at last, the blind reptile fell.

Mortally wounded, the surviving beast turned, hissing at the marines who had taken time to load their rifles. The volley fire crackled over the field and the reptile fell dead.

Dakkar dragged himself to his feet and stumbled over to Georgia, who was busy helping Blizzard up.

If it were possible, the man looked paler than ever. Dakkar winced at Blizzard's arm, seeing torn flesh, bone and muscle tissue exposed.

'I think I might lose that,' Blizzard said, grinning at Dakkar. 'Well done, lad. We did it.' And with that he collapsed backward on to the ground.

In the distance, the battle still raged on, the roar of men intensifying and cannon thundering in the background.

'The battle isn't finished,' Dakkar said, his voice quiet. 'Our part is done but only time will tell if Wellington can stop the French.'

'Just like to say, I admired the quick thinking on your part, sir,' one of the marines said to Dakkar, giving him a smart salute.

'It was an honour to fight alongside you, sir,' said another. He turned to Georgia. 'And you, miss.'

'Same to you.' Georgia gave a tight smile. 'I never thought I'd be saying that to a redcoat!'

They found some stray horses in the next field. Their saddlecloths and equipment identified them as French.

'Their riders shouldn't have been so careless as to leave 'em lyin' around,' said one of the marines, laughing.

Harnessing a horse to one of the remaining carts, they lay Blizzard down gently next to the boxes of arms and powder.

'We'll come back and clear the dead reptiles up when we've got the commander to a field hospital,' said a marine, taking one last look across the carnage.

Dakkar shook his head at all the death. The count was dead but he felt no elation – he just felt hollow.

They journeyed back towards the port in silence, nobody wanting to think about what they had just witnessed. Blizzard lay on the back of the cart, groaning at every bump and rut on the track. Finally, they found a small village church where red-coated soldiers stood sentry and blood-spattered orderlies hurried from table to table. Dakkar watched as they carried Blizzard into a side chapel.

'Looks nasty,' the doctor said. 'Caught in grapeshot or something? It looks chewed off.'

'Something like that,' Dakkar said, wincing. 'Will he be all right?'

'Who knows?' The doctor shook his head. 'We'll do our best but if it goes nasty on him, he's done for. The next twenty-four hours will tell.'

The orderlies hurried Dakkar and Georgia out of the church and Dakkar sat heavily on a barrel by the wooden doors.

'I really hope he pulls through,' Georgia said, laying a hand on Dakkar's shoulder.

'I don't know what to do.' Dakkar looked down at his boots. His whole body ached. 'I should rest but I can't help thinking about Oginski. I don't know if I should get back to Lyme or wait here for Blizzard.'

'We need to rest,' Georgia said. 'We can wait for twenty-four hours.'

Two of Blizzard's men stayed to guard him while Dakkar

and Georgia settled themselves in a barn not far from the church. Dakkar dozed in the straw, unable to sleep for thinking about Oginski and Blizzard and the events of the day.

It seemed late in the night when cheering woke Dakkar with a start. He and Georgia stumbled outside to see soldiers throwing their caps in the air and shaking hands. The cheering went on and one of Blizzard's marines came running from the church.

'Wellington has won, sir,' he shouted, his face beaming. 'Bonaparte is defeated!'

Dakkar grinned as Georgia threw her arms round him, then blushed as their faces came close, her cheek brushing his.

'So Cryptos has been thwarted once again.' Dakkar coughed and turned to the marine. 'And how is Commander Blizzard?'

The marine's face grew serious. 'Tolerably well, sir. They had to take his arm off. He's sleeping now.'

They found Blizzard sitting up in his makeshift bed the following morning. His body and the remainder of his arm were heavily bandaged. The church echoed with the groans of wounded men and Dakkar tried not to look too hard at the damaged soldiers scattered around this house of God.

'I knew they'd take my arm,' Blizzard said, sounding remarkably philosophical, if weak. 'Maybe you can make a mechanical one for me, Dakkar, with a fearsome hook at the end!'

'You have to rest now,' Georgia said, sitting next to the pallet bed, 'to avoid fever or infection.'

'I'll rest on HMS *Slaughter*, if it's all the same to you, young lady,' Blizzard said, raising an eyebrow. He scanned the church full of groaning, coughing soldiers. 'Lying around here won't improve my prospects one bit.'

The roads back to the port were clogged with troops returning and messengers flying back and forth, but somehow they managed to cut a path through them all.

Blizzard looked as though the faintest breeze would knock him flat but he sat on the cart, suppressing any sign of pain or discomfort.

'I never thought I'd be so glad to see Blizzard's ship,' Dakkar said when they finally reached the port.

Georgia nodded. 'Now we can get back to Lyme and Oginski.'

'I hope so,' Dakkar said in a quiet voice, looking up at Blizzard.

'You needn't worry about me,' Blizzard said. 'Once more, I am in your debt – and so is the King! Take your submersible and go home, but remember my offer for you to join Project Nemo – it's always open.'

Dakkar nodded. 'I'm grateful,' he said, 'but I'll be glad to get back to Cornwall and the castle.'

A blur of brown zipped through the air, squawks cutting above the rumble of carts and the shouts of men. Something flapped and squeaked above Dakkar's head.

'Gweek,' he said, holding out a hand and letting the reptile perch on it. 'Pleased to see me, eh?'

Mary hurried down the gangplank to meet them. 'Thank the Lord you're all right,' she said, clapping her hands. 'I heard the explosions from here. Was it terrible?'

'It was, but we're safe now,' Dakkar said, smiling. 'And we're going home!'

CHAPTER THIRTY-SIX
DEADLY LOOSE ENDS

The return journey across the English Channel proved uneventful. All the way back, Mary stared out of the portholes at the murky waters.

'Goin' to be strange to be back 'ome after all this time,' she said quietly.

'Hmm,' Georgia said, folding her arms and watching her. 'I think we *all* need to pay a visit to Oginski first.'

Mary had suggested beaching the *Liberty* close to the cave where the Ascender Cage had first taken her and Dakkar down to the underworld.

'It seemed pretty desolate,' Dakkar said, nodding. 'Can't be that well visited or else Cryptos wouldn't have put an entrance down there.'

'True,' said Georgia, twirling her hair in her fingers thoughtfully. 'Maybe that's why they never guarded it either.'

Once the *Liberty* was secured, the three of them hurried

up the beach towards Lyme. Dakkar panted, the sand dragging at his feet, the dread of what he might find pulling at his heart. *Please let him be alive, please!*

Daylight had barely grazed the twisting cobbled lanes as they clattered up them. Gweek settled on Dakkar's shoulder as they made their way up to Doctor Walbridge's house. A few curious fishermen turned their heads as the three ran past but carried on their way. Mary began to fall back but Georgia skidded to a halt and grabbed her by the elbow.

'Let me go!' Mary yelled.

'Georgia, what are you doing?' Dakkar said, frowning.

'She's coming with us,' Georgia snapped, whipping a pistol from under her jacket and pressing it to Mary's back.

'Have you gone mad?' Dakkar said, taking a step forward.

'Trust me,' Georgia said. 'I'm mad as hell!'

They walked on in silence, Mary's body shielding the pistol from the view of any passer-by.

'She just wants to see her mother,' Dakkar said, glancing over her shoulder. 'Do you have to march her at gunpoint to Oginski?' *If he's even alive!*

'I've a few questions I want to ask her before she goes anywhere,' Georgia said. 'Let's get to Doctor Walbridge.'

The doctor's house looked just as it had done when Dakkar left. He strode up to the door and rapped on it loudly. The door flew open and Cutter filled the entrance with his bulky frame.

'Dakkar!' he said, dragging him inside by the arm. 'You are a sight for sore eyes and no mistake!'

Mary entered next, followed by Georgia, pistol raised. Cutter's brow wrinkled in surprise and Georgia lowered the pistol.

'Oginski,' Dakkar said. 'Is he . . . all right?'

The doctor's living room looked crowded again with Cutter and the three new arrivals. Piper sat at the table along with Serge but there was no sign of the other men.

'He's fine,' Cutter said, his face relaxing. 'Weak but sitting up. Do you want to see him?'

'In a moment,' Georgia said, interrupting Dakkar's heartfelt response.

'Georgia?' Dakkar said. 'What's going on?'

'I suspect there is a traitor in our midst,' Georgia said, turning to Dakkar. She raised her pistol again. 'It's been bothering me ever since I first met Mary. How did you get down to the underworld?'

'Georgia, I told you,' Dakkar said, pointing to Mary. 'I followed her. How does that make her a traitor?'

'She's 'ad it in for me since we first met,' Mary said, sensing Dakkar's annoyance. 'I reckon she's jealous!'

'Jealous?' Dakkar murmured, scratching his head. *What would Georgia be jealous of?*

'And why were you following Mary?' Georgia tilted her head.

'To find out about the claw from Elba,' Dakkar said. 'I'd been told she might know about it.'

'Someone suggested you seek out Mary? Doesn't that

seem odd to you?' Georgia said. 'In the middle of all the chaos? Oginski is lying at death's door and someone feeds you Mary's name?'

'It weren't my idea,' Mary said, her face pale. She stared down at Piper. 'I was scared. I didn't wanna lead you down there.'

'Piper suggested I find Mary,' Dakkar gasped. 'He wanted me to follow her. They wanted to lure me down there. No wonder the Ascender Cage wasn't guarded!'

'What?' Piper looked up, his eyes wide.

'He caught me down there stealin' rocks,' Mary said, tears streaming down her face. 'He said he'd feed me to the lizards if I didn't do what he said –'

'Quiet, girl! You don't know what you're sayin',' Piper snapped, jumping up.

'It's true,' Mary sobbed. 'I'm not lyin'. I just want to go 'ome!'

'Piper, is this true?' Cutter said, his voice soft.

Piper lunged forward, turning the table over and knocking the gun from Georgia's hand. He punched Cutter, who staggered back into Serge. Seeing his chance, Piper barged past Dakkar and ran for the door. Straight into the barrel of a gun.

'I wouldn't move if I were you, Mr Piper,' said a familiar voice.

'Oginski!' Dakkar yelled.

Oginski stood, leaning on a cane but holding a pistol firmly to Piper's head. He looked thinner, greyer and wore a dressing gown, but it was Oginski all right.

'Hello, Dakkar,' he said, giving a feeble grin. 'What have you been up to?'

Dakkar, Georgia and Oginski sat in Walbridge's living room. Although it was summer, Oginski had asked for a fire and it was clear from his lined face that his recovery had been slow. After some deliberation, Mary had been sworn to secrecy and returned to her mother.

'Don't you worry,' she'd said, having regained her composure after Piper's attempted escape. 'I'm stickin' to the top side beaches from now on.'

Cutter and Serge took Piper back to Cutter's Cove.

'What will they do with him?' Dakkar shuddered as he watched them disappear down the cobbled lane.

'Cryptos's justice is rough and final,' Oginski murmured, his eyes fixed on Cutter's back. 'That's between them. But if they don't think they can trust him . . .' Oginski shrugged.

'So much death,' Dakkar whispered. 'It was horrible down there in the underworld but the battlefield was even worse.'

Oginski nodded. 'Man is by far the more savage beast.' But you saw great sacrifice and courage too. You saw true leaders who care about their fellow men.'

'I did,' Dakkar agreed, thinking of Gog and Bonaparte and Blizzard. 'Your brother ruled by fear – and lusted after power, which was his downfall.'

'You won a battle this time,' Oginski said, the news of another brother's death etched in his drawn face. 'But other battles will unfold before us . . .'

'Other battles?' Georgia said, frowning.

'My brothers don't rest,' Oginski sighed, staring into the fire. 'Schemes will have been hatched already – I have no doubt of that. Maybe Blizzard and his Project Nemo will prove a useful ally. Who knows?'

'But we do have each other,' Dakkar said, grabbing Georgia and Oginski's hands, 'and nothing can stop us!'

A NOTE FROM THE AUTHOR

I took inspiration for *The Wrath of the Lizard Lord* from one of Jules Verne's great stories, *Journey to the Centre of the Earth*. In Verne's book, there is a world beneath our feet populated by prehistoric creatures and giant cavemen – although the heroes in his book merely observe these creatures and certainly don't blow any up! In some translations, the cavemen are huge, fierce gorillas; in others, they're more human.

1815 was a year of world-changing events. The armies of Napoleon Bonaparte met those of the Duke of Wellington at the Battle of Waterloo in June. Wellington was said to declare that victory wasn't certain for him, even though Bonaparte had been defeated once already. Napoleon is often characterised as a power-hungry tyrant but there were plenty of people who saw him as a liberator from oppressive monarchs and as a symbol of freedom. After Waterloo, Napoleon was captured and imprisoned on the island of St Helena until his death. Many conspiracy theories surround his time there. It is alleged that Napoleon's most loyal soldiers planned to rescue him using a submarine! It is also said that he employed doubles in dangerous situations. One theory suggests that the man who died on St Helena was in fact one of these doubles and that the real Napoleon died in Austria, but there is no hard evidence to prove this.

When I was young, like any small boy, I was fascinated by dinosaurs, and the chance to write about them was too good to miss. My father was a keen fossil hunter and my early beach holidays involved scouring shores and cliffs for ammonites and petrified coral. Mary Anning hunted fossils for a living. She was credited with discovering the first complete ichthyosaur and plesiosaur skeletons and is an important figure in the development of palaeontology. She was a remarkable person, who apparently survived being struck by lightning as a baby. Her father died when she was eleven, forcing her to make a living collecting fossils and selling them to holidaymakers. Throughout her life, she assisted notable scientists in the study and assembly of fossil specimens and sold many samples all over the world. Collecting fossils could be a dangerous occupation – Mary was nearly buried alive when a cliff above her collapsed while she was out searching.

In 1815, the term 'dinosaur' hadn't even been thought up. This presented me with the problem of what to call the creatures in my book. I couldn't use modern names such as Tyrannosaurus rex or brontosaurus, so I decided to call them by the names the giants used. Basically, if it flies, it's a Gacheela; if it eats meat, it's a Saranda; and the bipeds that the Cryptos Guard ride are called Rohaga. I thought it might be more fun for you to get your dinosaur books out, read my descriptions and decide for yourself exactly what kind of dinosaur you might ride!

Look out for the next instalment of
Monster Odyssey, coming 2015

Also available in this series: *Monster Odyssey: The Eye of Neptune*

Prince Dakkar, heir to an Indian kingdom, has been expelled from
the best schools in England. Now he's stuck with the mysterious
Count Oginski, genius inventor of a top-secret machine:
the world's first submersible.

But in a dangerous world of spies and secrecy, someone would
do anything to capture Oginski's invention. When the count is
kidnapped, Dakkar escapes in the submarine, only to face horrifying
creatures of the deep, lethal giant squid and, above all, the sinister
Cryptos, who is hell-bent on taking over the world . . .

And don't miss . . .

Edgy Taylor sees demons when nobody else can. They disguise themselves as humans, but Edgy knows the truth and it's driving him crazy. So when he learns of a Royal Society for Daemonologie, Edgy hopes to discover the reason for his strange talent.

Necessity Bonehill has unleashed an evil djinn from his bottle. Now she has just seven days to put him back. But the djinn has a different plan, and returning to his prison of three thousand years isn't part of it.

. . . or Mortlock

Josie is a knife thrower in a magician's stage act. Alfie is an undertaker's assistant. They are both orphans and they have never met, but they are about to be given a clue to the secret of their shared past. A past which has come to seek them out.

And while they flee for their lives, they must unravel the burning mysteries surrounding the legacy that threatens to consume them.